'Jane...' he whispered huskily, his breath fanning over her cheek. 'Oh, Jane, have we changed that much from the people we used to be?'

'I suppose now...I...I'm a little set in my ways...' she answered with brutal honesty as she stared up at him. 'I've only myself to think about.'

'And you've never wanted a family—children of your own?'

How could she explain how she had been forced to smother those longings without laying the blame for what had happened at his feet? Of course she had wanted babies—*his* babies. Expecting to marry Marcus herself, she had dreamed of a family of their own.

'Oh, Marcus...you don't understand—'

'Then make me understand,' he growled as his lips sought hers, and the kiss they shared was intense and deep, his tongue seeking the sweetness of her mouth, his hands pulling her against him...

Join the
Country Partners
in these two fabulous linked titles by Carol Wood:

Meet the partners in this lively, rural practice.
In this bustling community, nestled in the heart
of Dorset, the Doctors of the Nair Surgery
are kept busy with the trials and tribulations
of their patients, friends and colleagues.

But can they find time for their own lives, and loves?
Will these country partners, become partners—for life?

THE HONOURABLE DOCTOR
Discover whether Dr Marcus Granger
and Dr Jane Court can rekindle their love...

and in
October 2001
THE PATIENT DOCTOR
Will Cenna be able to convince the
irresistible Dr Phil Granger to love again?

Country Partners
Care in the community—love in the surgery.

THE HONOURABLE DOCTOR

BY
CAROL WOOD

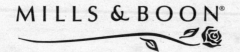

MILLS & BOON®

First published in Great Britain 2001
Harlequin Mills & Boon Limited,
Eton House, 18-24 Paradise Road, Richmond, Surrey TW9 1SR

© Carol Roma Wood 2001

ISBN 0 263 82670 8

Set in Times Roman 10½ on 11½ pt.
03-0601-52341

Printed and bound in Spain
by Litografia Rosés, S.A., Barcelona

CHAPTER ONE

JANE wrinkled her small nose against the wind-whipped pane of glass as the unseasonal easterly gale howled around Nair's tightly battened roofs.

'Early April and it could be November,' she sighed to herself as she tried to overcome the feeling of seasonal disorientation which had firmly encapsulated the small coastal town. 'Whatever next, I wonder...'

Her thoughts returned to Maggie Jardine's accident last Christmas, then the stricken tanker in March, now spring and the outbreak of flu. And still the storms raged, turning the calm blue waters that normally flowed around Nair's sandy shores into a cauldron of angry grey turbulence.

One brave shaft of sunlight broke from the bruised sky and caused Jane to widen her clear blue eyes in hopeful anticipation. She lifted her face to the warmth, her long, naturally blonde hair falling back from fine, sensitive features, the wrinkle of irritation on her brow fading as she took in a deep breath. Salt, sea and the promise of spring...

A smile touched her lips as the breeze whistled through a gap in the window-frame, reminding her of the plans for the new surgery. Well under way, it was only a matter of finalising a few details, most of which Phil had dealt with. Not that it had been easy for the senior partner after his wife's death...

Turning to find Paula Locke staring at her with more than a little candour in her expression, Jane's eyebrows arched in an expressive curve. 'Let me guess what you've got there.' She grinned as she eased her slender body into the leather seat behind her desk and accepted the paperwork.

'Headache, sickness, temperature, chest infection and probably a touch of arthritis—and what else? Maybe sun deficiency combined with a nasty rash…'

'You should be so lucky,' laughed the receptionist, a slim, fair-headed young woman who wagged a finger in the air. 'You'll have to be patient for those goodies, Dr Court. First, you've a nice little appetiser—an appointment that hasn't been marked in the book or put on the computer. And our man is very insistent he made the appointment for eleven this morning.'

'Oh, lucky me,' Jane sighed, closing her eyes in mock despair, her blonde lashes sweeping over a sprinkling of freckles which had stubbornly refused to fade throughout winter. As she lifted them, the sea-blue pools of colour that swirled there caused Paula Locke to giggle.

'You might have a pleasant surprise, actually, Dr Court. He's a candidate for the locum's job and he *is* rather scrumptious. And as a new recruit he would certainly add to the decor. Still, mustn't get our hopes up, must we—bearing in mind the other two.'

Jane didn't need reminding of the previous applicants for the locum's post. Both had rushed eagerly into the surgery and just as eagerly out again. She had been unable to give either of them the time of day as all hell had let loose when the beleaguered tanker had broken up in the bay. The prospective interviewees had left with little more than vague promises to return.

And who could blame them? The picturesque coastal hamlet of the holiday brochures had provided them with the most unwelcoming prospect possible—a sea trauma, gale-force winds, a media frenzy and three GPs caught up in the resulting turmoil. Not forgetting a senior partner who had just suffered his own personal bereavement.

'So, shall I send him in, Dr Court?' Paula was saying as

Jane lifted her distracted gaze. Aware that she hadn't even opened the CV in front of her, Jane nodded.

'Wheel him in, Paula. And when Dr Jardine comes in from his calls, tell him I'm interviewing our candidate.' She added with a wry smile, 'That is, if Dr Jardine should ask.'

'Skipped his mind, I expect. Shan't bother to say if he doesn't mention it. And if we do hook our man, it will be a nice surprise for him, won't it?' The receptionist shrugged good-naturedly as she left and Jane smiled gratefully. The staff had been wonderful with Phil, smoothing over all the cracks and lapses of memory. Everyone had felt his loss keenly and would have gone to the ends of the earth to help him through it.

Jane stroked down her suit top thoughtfully, the fine blue linen more appropriate for a summer's day than torrential rain and wind. Luckily she had worn something decent, but the mood of rebellion she had woken in after such a wet Easter had been fortuitous in this case. Trousers and a jumper might just have thrown away her chances of impressing the man.

Not that she was ashamed of her surroundings, far from it. The old building might be lacking in amenities but the warmth of all the staff made up for any shortcomings. The girls on Reception were a great team and Cenna Lloyd, at twenty-eight the youngest doctor of the partnership, had become a close friend as well as a valued colleague. Everyone shared Phil's optimism for the future, certain that when the plans for the new surgery were finalised new Nair Surgery would be just as successful as the old one had been.

Dr Jardine senior had pioneered the surgery, and when he had died ten years ago, Phil had stepped into his father's shoes, maintaining the same warmth and affection towards his patients as his father before him.

Jane sighed softly, turning the pages of the folder in front of her, but her mind still dwelt on the past. Only last year Phil had had so much to look forward to—his brainchild, the new premises and its opening scheduled for the New Year. Then, sadly, his wife's tragic death abroad in a skiing accident just before Christmas had meant everything had been put on hold.

Jane gave herself a sharp mental shake. Phil would come through this testing time and, at only thirty-one, she herself had much to give. She wouldn't let him down. She owed him too much. She owed Nair too much!

Her gaze travelled to the window once again as a faint whistle of wind echoed from the crevice. The wall of the crofter's cottage might be old and weary, but she loved every creaking rafter, every draughty window. Nair Surgery had opened its doors to her at the darkest time in her life and she would never forget the debt she owed it.

'Dr Court, this is Dr Granger. Would you like me to bring you some coffee? Or tea? There's no one waiting, so it won't be a problem...' Paula's bright voice broke into her thoughts and Jane turned slowly to meet the deep grey gaze of the tall man standing beside the receptionist.

In one shattering moment all thoughts were erased from Jane's mind as the carefully erected defences of the last seven years crumbled away like so much sand under a rushing tide.

'Dr Court?' Hesitantly Paula stepped forward as she repeated her question.

With an effort that cost Jane far more than she allowed herself to admit, she rose to her feet and nodded. 'Yes...yes, coffee, thank you, Paula.'

The young receptionist's frown was still in place as she left the room, and the door closed quietly behind her. Jane's heart pounded in her chest as her suit felt suddenly constrictive around her chest. Her legs had lost all sensation, a faint sickness swelling and retreating at the pit of her stomach—all symptoms she recognised with the professional side of her brain of shock.

However, her visitor appeared to suffer no such symptoms. Calm, silver-grey eyes stared back at her under a shock of windswept black hair, a pelt of thick ebony that framed the same lived-in, engraved face that she remembered from the past. A face that could have been sculpted from bronze, beaten and honed from the hardest of metals, yet had a surprisingly mobile beauty. Grainy skin flawlessly smoothed over hard, intractable bone. A face that she had gazed on for so many hours, days and years, in lust and love and, finally, in despair.

'Jane?' His voice rumbled across the room and the sound of it had her sucking in her breath, holding herself tightly, fists bunched, breath gathered in as her head reeled crazily.

Too late she resisted his help as strong arms gathered her as she crumpled, the blackness obliterating thoughts as the whirlpool of dizziness triumphed over even the howl of the storm outside. Somewhere in her brain she knew he was holding her and somewhere she was still resisting, the nausea flowing up into her throat and subsiding again.

Her lids flickered open to find him down on one knee, squeezing her hand tightly, his thumbs rubbing gently over her knuckles. 'My God, Jane, you gave me a fright. Aren't you well?'

She leaned forward on the chair, unable to protest at the curve of his strong arm around her, smelling on the navy-blue cashmere overcoat the sensual, earthy tang of cologne that, blindfolded, she could have identified as Marcus Granger. 'I…I'm fine. Please, don't fuss. I'll be all right.'

'Don't fuss?' he growled in apparent surprise. 'What the heck are you talking about, Jane? What do you expect, fainting on me like that? What's happened to you?'

'N-nothing. I…I skipped breakfast, that's all,' she answered weakly, not daring to lift her eyes to his. 'Please, Marcus, let me go.'

But the arm around her and the long, strong fingers refused to move. A low, guttural sound rasped in his throat as he shook his head. 'Things haven't changed much, have they? I always used to have to force-feed you in the mornings. Look at the size of you. How much weight have you lost, girl?'

It was this demand that brought her round quicker than a bucket of cold water thrown in her face. She pushed herself back and out of his grip, blinking furiously to rid herself of the little black flecks dancing across her vision. 'My weight gain—or loss—has been of no interest to you for the last seven years,' she thrust at him in a disembodied voice. 'I hardly think you need display concern now.' Using all her will-power, she tried to stand up.

'And still as stubborn,' her visitor added, drawing a breath as he rose to his feet, too, shoulders hunched under the expensive cashmere coat. 'For heaven's sake, be careful—at least have a drink of water.'

Casting her eyes up once more, she managed a scornful glare and then made her way unsteadily to the washbasin in the corner of the room. Grasping the sink, she forced back her concentration. What a fool she was making of herself. She needed time—just a few moments to gather herself.

Taking a glass from the shelf, she turned on the tap and water grumbled from it, the ancient plumbing system thankfully filling the uncomfortable silence. The coolness was like balm to her throat and she gulped it down, straightening her back and blinking rapidly.

'Better?' asked the concerned voice behind her.

Still refusing to turn to meet his gaze, she nodded abruptly, at the same time catching her reflection in the mirror and despairing at the sight. A white, shocked face, the startled blue of her eyes accentuating her pallor. Only the crown of shining blonde hair curving softly into a bob around her face hid the truth that the mirror revealed.

He was right, of course. She had lost weight. But it was a long time ago that heartache and loneliness had changed for ever the ample proportions of the young medical student Marcus Granger had once known.

She pulled back her shoulders determinedly and, taking one last thirsty sip, she returned the glass to the shelf, her shaking fingers reluctant to leave its solid coolness. Turning slowly, she prepared to look at him, but this time, she promised herself, she would keep firmly in control, no matter what the effort cost her.

'Would you like me to come back at a more…convenient time?' Marcus's question came as she reclaimed her chair behind her desk. The atmosphere was tense as she made herself comfortable, lifting her eyes only when she was certain of regained self-control.

'No, that won't be necessary.' Opening the blue folder in front of her, she at once took in the details she had omitted to digest before his arrival. Training and qualification at a top London hospital—the same hospital at which she and Katrina had also been based. His final year and the subtle omission of any personal details in the text until two years later.

She looked up slowly. 'Why have you come here, Marcus?'

Broad shoulders shrugged dismissively as he settled back in the chair. Self-assurance radiated around him. Under the cashmere coat was the same disarmingly confident man she had once known, a burning energy seeming to fill every muscle in his tall, lean frame.

'Personal reasons,' he replied in a gravel voice that had lost none of its deep resonance over the intervening years. 'I simply saw the advertisement, thought the post would suit my current circumstances—and wrote. Phillip Jardine rang me a week or so ago. By the time I learned you were here…' Tilting his head slightly, he frowned, adding in a low tone, 'I'd arranged to come for the interview. I thought it over and decided if there were any…' He paused again, as if searching for the right word. 'Any *objections*…to my appearance, they would surface beforehand. I waited, but no one rang me. And so here I am—though I have to say your receptionist seemed slightly surprised to see me this morning.'

Jane realised that Paula had done her best to cover for Phil's mistake. And what would she—Jane—have done if she had known it had been Marcus Granger applying? Would she have voiced her objections to Phil? Would she have tried to block Marcus from an interview?

'This *is* a temporary post,' she faltered as she tried to gain time, 'just until we move to the new premises—'

'Where you'll have a greater choice in candidates for a permanent position?' he interrupted, one eyebrow raised sardonically. 'Yes, I'm aware of the small print. I assure you, I'm not trying to muscle my way in on your new practice. Six months, nine months, whatever, is fine by me.'

Her mind raced. 'In other words, you have plans for the future…and Nair would be a stop-gap?' she pressed cautiously.

Again the broad shoulders rose in a dismissive shrug. 'Ben is my first consideration. I'm hoping the sea air will help alleviate his asthma—not helped by the air quality in the city.'

Averting her gaze to the CV, she tried to reassemble her confused thoughts. He seemed to be genuine in his reasons for coming to Nair. Added to which he had the disconcerting ability to force her into another uncomfortable admission.

'I…I'm sorry to hear that,' she murmured, her eyes coming up slowly to meet his. 'I…I didn't know.'

'How could you?' His eyes were accusing. 'You disappeared from the scene overnight. You left no forwarding address, nothing at all.'

She swallowed, emotion cloying her throat as she stared at the man sitting opposite her, and for a heart-stopping moment she was tempted to confess the real reason she had fled from him.

But the temptation was short-lived. If she had kept secret Katrina's growing suspicion and hostility all these years, she would not reveal it now when, long after Katrina's death, it would seem even more like a betrayal of their friendship.

'Obviously you knew about Katrina's death?' Marcus's voice was bereft of emotion.

She nodded. 'Yes,' she responded in a voice so low that she was forced—revealingly—to clear her throat, blinking on the sudden mist in her eyes. She had, indeed, read the obituary eighteen months later, recognising Katrina's name.

She had considered going to the funeral but had decided against it. Her emotions had still been too raw, she had still been too vulnerable. The only way she had come to terms with Katrina's change in attitude after her marriage to Marcus had been by telling herself that she, too, would have felt the same way had the positions been reversed. And even though Katrina had made an effort, Jane had known that she had no longer been welcome at their home.

Finally, on that beautiful summer's evening seven years ago, she had taken the final step, leaving them to their only chance of happiness throughout the remainder of Katrina's short life.

'I think,' Marcus said suddenly, pushing back his chair, 'that it was wrong of me to come.' His eyes met hers and she felt herself drowning in them. What could she say—

where could she begin? Her thoughts were in turmoil and she panicked afresh, her mouth opening slowly as she fought to find the right words.

But before she could reply he was on his feet, pushing a tired hand up over his chin and into his hair. 'Look, I'm sorry…this isn't helping either of us.' He hugged his coat closer to him, his broad shoulders bent momentarily before the grey eyes lifted. 'Coming here wasn't such a good idea after all…'

Her heart seemed to jump in her chest as she tried again to form words, her lips trembling as she called out to stop him. But no words came as he disappeared into the corridor, leaving the overwhelming silence of the empty room behind him.

As Jane sat there, the past came flooding back, a stream of vivid mental pictures—her childhood, growing up on her parents' farm in the Midlands, leaving college for London and her first meeting with Katrina Davidson at the London hospital where they were to train.

She'd made friends with Katrina at once. A dark, pretty girl with a reserved manner, Katrina's background had not been dissimilar to her own. Both from the Midlands, they had immediately hit it off. Each had been determined to qualify and had Katrina not met James Conway, perhaps she would have achieved that ambition. Perhaps…

Jane felt her head swim as Katrina's face appeared in her mind. With Marcus's appearance in her life again, her defences seemed to have crumbled and she was shocked at her recollection of Katrina. Health and confidence radiated from her elfin features. Gone was the sick, distraught girl who had begged her and Marcus for help. Only the lovely young student remained, her bright, dark eyes full of her dreams for the future.

The vision of a tall, stunningly handsome young Marcus appeared then—two years ahead of her and Katrina, Marcus and his friend James Conway had gravitated towards the first-year students shyly ogling them at a hospital party. Katrina had been smitten with James at once, but her own attraction to Marcus had developed more slowly. Those had been the happy times and those which now came back to mind, despite all the sadness that was to follow.

But if Jane thought only the happy memories remained she was wrong. Emotions that had really never been buried followed hard on the heels of recall. The dreadful heartache, which for seven years she had fought and triumphed over, now filled her anew. Katrina's pregnancy, her desperate cry for help, Marcus's and Katrina's wedding—and baby Ben. All pictures returning vividly to mind, and with the recollections the sensations of separation and ultimate loss.

Jane felt her body tremble as she clutched the desk. She didn't want to remember these emotions. She had called upon every reserve to fight them. That part of her life was over. She couldn't open that box again.

'Jane!' The exclamation burst into her consciousness and she blinked hard, recognising the voice, as the unwelcome ghosts in her mind were suddenly put to flight. 'Jane—you must think I'm an idiot. *Jane…?*'

Suddenly a face appeared before her. 'Phil? Phil…you're back…'

Phillip Jardine, senior partner of Nair Surgery, was standing in front of her, and beside him was Marcus Granger.

'I've explained to Marcus,' Phil was saying in a rush, his dark eyes appealing silently to her, 'it was my fault entirely. My fault. How can it have slipped my mind?'

Marcus stood with hands thrust deeply into his coat pockets. His unsmiling face told her all she wanted to know. He said abruptly, 'Phil, you've a waiting room full to the brim out there. I'll see your receptionist, make another time perhaps—'

'I wouldn't hear of it!' Phil interjected, his horrified gaze once more swinging back to Jane for support. A tall, dark-haired man with harrowed features, the bereavement he had suffered six months ago was still clearly etched on his face. 'We're both delighted to have the opportunity to talk to you, aren't we, Jane?'

She had no alternative but to nod, then, glancing back at the slightly taller of the two men, she began, 'Though it might not be convenient for Dr Granger, Phil.'

'I do have my son waiting outside,' Marcus agreed shortly. 'It's been a long morning and I need to feed Ben before driving back to London.'

'No problem,' Phil protested desperately. 'Let me show you around the practice—Paula and Annie, our two recep-tionists, will keep your lad occupied until we're done. Then I'll drive all of us into Nair for some lunch.' Phillip lifted his dark eyebrows. 'I really do want to correct the abysmal first impression I've made, Marcus.'

Phillip Jardine had faced so many crises in the last few months and Jane reflected sadly as she listened that he seemed to be clutching at straws here. This was also evident to Marcus, she could see, as his hesitation lengthened into an uncomfortable silence.

'Phil, I really would like to, but—' he began eventually, only to be stopped by a loud explosion that seemed to shake the foundations of the building.

'What in heaven's name was that?' Phil exclaimed as they all moved toward the door.

Cenna Lloyd, the younger female partner of Nair Sur-gery, hurried from her room towards them. 'There's been an accident on the hill,' she called breathlessly, her face ashen under her long, dark hair. 'I can see the two cars from my window. They must have collided.'

Jane went onto autopilot then, meeting the younger female doctor's glance with a brief nod. Grabbing her coat and case, she sprinted from the room, Phil just ahead of her and Marcus at her side.

CHAPTER TWO

DR CENNA LLOYD shivered in the wind, drawing her jacket around her slim shoulders. The paramedics finally removed the unconscious young man on the stretcher to the ambulance. Marcus Granger, the doctor who had arrived for an interview, nodded to her as he rolled down his sleeves and shrugged on his coat.

As he talked to the policeman, she transferred her gaze to the wreck of one of the vehicles. Both drivers had been speeding as they'd driven in opposite directions over the brow of the hill. Neither driver had had time to stop as Mr Macauley had hobbled slowly across the road on his Zimmer. Miraculously, the eighty-two-year-old had survived unscathed. Hard of hearing and very short-sighted, the pensioner now sat with Jane in the surgery, refusing to go to hospital.

The police had ringed off the road, for a while diverting traffic. They were waiting for the recovery vehicle to arrive, and the orange tape and road signs were clear evidence to other drivers of the recent misfortune. The young man had suffered multiple injuries and it was Marcus Granger who had attended to him, applying the neck support and setting up the drip before the ambulance arrived.

Cenna had been impressed by his calm, efficient manner. Removing his coat, he had worked in the howling wind as he'd attended the severely injured young man trapped in his car. She and Phillip had seen to the three people in the hatchback which had come to a halt on a grass verge, its bodywork demolished on impact.

The female driver was amazingly uninjured, though trau-

18

matised. One man had broken a leg, the other had sustained
a back injury. The strong winds had done nothing to help
conditions, neither had the cramped space in the crushed
Volvo in which they had been forced to work.

The emergency services had cut free the young man, and
all the accident victims were now on their way to
Southampton General. All that was left to do was to persuade Mr Macauley, blissfully unaware that an accident had
occurred, never to attempt a journey on foot to the surgery
again. But the elderly man was stubborn. Cenna doubted
that even Jane would have much luck.

A fact borne out as she turned from the windswept road
to see Jane and Annie helping Mr Macauley into a taxi. It
looked as though Annie was accompanying the old man
home as she also climbed in. Cenna sighed once more. If
she knew Mr Macauley, this whole episode would probably
sail over his head.

Burrowing down into her jacket, she hurried towards the
crofter's cottage that was Nair Surgery. The whitewashed
walls glistened in the weak sunshine, a line of gulls perched
uniformly on the roof. A sprinkling of cottages behind
broke the gentle slope of the hillside down to Nair itself.
Set in a lush green valley, with a dozen slate roofs glinting
in the waning sun, Nair could be forgiven for much during
the summer months.

As she hugged herself tightly, Cenna bent low against
the wind. Would Marcus Granger take the post of locum?
she wondered. After the accident and the unfortunate mix-
up on interview times, which she had learned of from Phil,
would he consider the position two candidates had already
turned down?

Even she herself had second thoughts about her work at
times, especially in the harsh, windy winters. But on a true
summer's day Nair was magical. And the new premises,

built in the centre of Nair itself, would offer so much more scope when completed.

Cenna looked up from her thoughts to find Jane coming towards her. Jane's blonde head was also bowed against the wind; tall and reed-slender, her long legs moved quickly under her beige, calf-length winter coat.

'Any luck with Mr Macauley?' Cenna called against the wind.

'None at all,' Jane shrugged as they met, her windswept blonde hair whirling across her cheeks. 'He wouldn't believe there was an accident, let alone that he was the cause of it. Annie bravely volunteered to see him home.'

Cenna nodded, attempting to tuck down her own long dark hair into the collar of her coat. She brushed its thickness back from her large amber-coloured eyes, suddenly feeling the energy drain out of her.

'Cenna, you look frozen,' Jane murmured, reaching for her arm. 'Come on in. How was the young man?'

Cenna shrugged as they walked together. 'Multiple internal injuries, so Marcus fears.' She paused, glancing at Jane again. 'That is his name, isn't it—Marcus Granger?'

Jane nodded, her head down, but she said nothing.

'He was very impressive, you know,' Cenna continued. 'Calm and unruffled, but he worked amazingly quickly on that young driver's injuries.'

Again Jane remained silent and Cenna wondered why she didn't respond. Neither Jane nor Marcus had spoken to one another. It appeared almost as if they'd addressed their comments deliberately to other people. However, under the circumstances, perhaps she was mistaken.

'You're shaking like a leaf,' Jane said quickly as another gust of wind almost took them off their feet. 'I'll get Paula to make us all a hot drink.'

'I'm sure Marcus could do with one. But he's still talking to the police,' Cenna replied, glancing over her shoulder.

Both the cold and the shock of the accident were getting to her and she hesitated, dreading to think how frozen their new candidate must be.

'Well, I'm sure he'll cope. Let's get you fixed up first,' Jane answered, pulling her on. 'There are three of your patients still hanging on, but the others went home after making new appointments. To be honest, I don't think anyone felt like hanging around after the accident.'

Somewhat surprised by Jane's indifference to the poor man's situation, Cenna shuddered with relief as they walked into the small, warm waiting room. The bright sea prints on the whitewashed walls always reminded her of the cottage's sea origins. They had done everything to make the place cosy, but the surgery was far too cramped now and she really looked forward to moving. However, when that would now be she couldn't guess, and she gave herself up to the slightly claustrophobic feeling of the old surgery.

Her patients were sitting on the comfortable rattan chairs and sofas that filled the waiting room—Brian Jeffrey, the builder, Leonora Crawley, a teacher at the primary school and Clyde Oakman, a local fisherman.

Cenna followed Jane to the desk where Paula looked up, a phone in one hand, a pen in the other. Beyond her in the office a small boy was curled up in the easy chair, his eyes glued to the television.

'Our one concession to luxury seems to be doing the trick.' Paula grinned as she followed Cenna's interested gaze. 'Cable TV and Disney for the kids.'

'Which patient does he belong to?' Cenna asked, just beginning to feel the warmth pervade her frozen skin.

'Not patient, Dr Lloyd. He's Marcus Granger's son, Ben. And he's gorgeous. I told him to watch the TV while his dad was occupied outside. He did what he was told, though I think the bang shook him up a bit. Annie took him a drink earlier and put his mind at rest that his dad would be in soon.' Paula frowned at Cenna. 'I hear it was pretty bad out there on the road. Are you all right? Can I make you a coffee?'

Cenna nodded, her attention distracted by the little boy. 'Whenever you're ready, Paula. No rush. I'm fine.' Turning to Jane, she was shocked to find her colleague walking quickly away as Marcus, windswept and hunched, entered the surgery.

'You must be mistaken, Doctor, I never sunbathe.'

Jane frowned at the assortment of blotches on her patient's face, chest and legs and diplomatically reserved judgement. 'Well, these may be nothing, but I'd like to attend to this area here first on your chest. As for removing the smaller sites on your legs—'

'*Remove* them!' Nancy Farlow exclaimed, as she sat up on the examination bench and stared disbelievingly at Jane. 'But I've had these moles for years. You can't be serious, Dr Court.'

'Well, you've had some bleeding from this one.' Jane indicated the area below her patient's bra. 'And the lesion here, on your chest, looks slightly inflamed around the edges. It looks as though you may have had some irritation—'

'I probably scratched it in my sleep,' the woman said defensively, quickly pulling on her jumper. 'Honestly, if I was a sun worshipper, I could understand it. But the only time I ever went in the sun was when I worked for my firm in Australia.'

'When were you there and for how long?' Jane asked, returning to her desk.

'Oh, years ago!' Nancy Farlow patted her chignon back into place. 'When I was in my twenties. I lived there for about five or six years.'

Jane looked up at the sophisticated, middle-aged blonde

woman with astute bright blue eyes dressed in a grey power suit. A marketing executive and commuter to the City, she rarely attended the surgery. Her annual check was her only visit and Jane had always been pleased to give her a clean bill of health. However, on this occasion she was hesitant to allow her patient to leave without making a further appointment.

'It won't take very long to remove the suspect areas,' Jane said lightly. 'I'll do it for you, if you prefer, in the small ops surgery we have on Wednesdays.'

'What happens when you remove them?' Nancy Farlow buttoned up the jacket of her suit and sat in the patient's chair. 'Is that it?'

'No. We send the specimen for analysis. The biopsy results are pretty quick. You can ring in from work and speak to me. Give it a week or so and I should have received them by then.'

Ms Nancy Farlow sighed. 'I really don't have the time for this, Dr Court. I'm under pressure at work to complete a staff assessment. Couldn't all this wait?'

Jane wondered just what was preventing Nancy from making a further appointment. She was an intelligent woman and there had been enough media coverage on skin cancers in the UK to alert any thinking person to the possibilities. Her patient was fair-skinned, blue-eyed and over forty. She had been exposed to strong sunlight in her youth and the ulcerated areas that Jane had discovered had certainly not been there last year or she would have noticed them. She would have expected more co-operation from a woman like Nancy Farlow.

'Come and see me again in the next couple of weeks or so,' Jane suggested. 'Perhaps the Wednesday after next? If you can make the last appointment of the day—say five-thirty—it won't interfere too much with your busy schedule.'

Nancy Farlow laughed as she stood up. 'My schedule at the moment, Dr Court, is a nightmare. I'm never home before ten these days. My department is very stressed.'

This was a familiar story, Jane reflected, though she made no comment. But nothing was more important than health—and it was, after all, why her patient came to see her each year.

'But I'll do as you ask,' her patient complied, lifting the briefcase that was on the floor beside her. 'See you in two weeks, then. And I'm afraid it will have to be your last appointment of the day. I hope your receptionist can arrange that. From the horror stories you see on TV these days, appointments are few and far between.'

'I'll ring through to Reception and explain to Paula.' Jane smiled wryly. 'You won't have any trouble.'

'I don't know whether that's good news or bad,' said her patient with a grin as she left, but Jane wasn't fooled by her carefree manner. Nancy Farlow, to all intents and purposes, was a formidable career woman who had always enjoyed good health. Jane wondered how her patient would react to something beyond her immediate control. She sighed, dropping her chin into her hands and resting it there for a few moments.

'May I come in?' The voice at the door broke into her thoughts and she looked up to see Marcus standing there.

She nodded, sitting slowly back in her chair, tiredness sweeping over her. It had been a long day. The shock of seeing Marcus had dulled now and she was resigned—almost—to the fact that she had no way of avoiding him.

'I thought you and I had better talk—that is, if you've finished surgery?'

Again she nodded, gesturing to the chair. 'Yes, I'm finished.' She looked beyond him. 'Where's Ben?'

'Fast asleep in front of the television,' he told her with a rueful smile. It was the first time he had really smiled and the lopsided twist of lips brought back another wave of memories. He had always had a wonderful smile... Whenever he had come into a room, she had known that smile had been just for her. Jane felt her heart race and she looked away, shuffling Nancy Farlow's records into order.

'One satisfied customer?' remarked Marcus as he sat down, his long legs encased in smart grey trousers, his jacket slightly open, revealing an expanse of white shirt which Annie had earlier dabbed clean. The accident debris and blood which had soiled it earlier in the day had been efficiently disposed of with the help of an ingenious stain-remover.

Despite the earlier events, Marcus looked cool and collected. Very little had changed about him, Jane found herself thinking. He had always dressed well, with impeccable taste, though perhaps always in an understated way. Nothing had ever seemed to ruffle him...

'I'm afraid not.' She shook her head slowly. 'Not at all satisfied, I'm afraid. In fact, I'm a little concerned at her reaction. I just hope I can convince her to follow up our discussion with treatment.'

It was evident his concern was genuine as his tone resumed a sober note. 'Once again I seem to have arrived at the wrong time.'

'No,' Jane answered, meeting his gaze. 'It's just been a very long day.'

An awkward silence settled between them as he watched her carefully. 'Look, Jane, you're obviously not comfortable with my presence here...'

'What did you expect?' Her voice was low and brusque. She wasn't doing a very good job of hiding her feelings, she knew.

'I don't know what I expected, to be perfectly honest,' he answered her quietly. 'All I can tell you is I thought that if there were strong objections on your part, you'd make it plain enough to Phil. I would have understood and kept away. As I understand it now, it was by mistake that I succeeded in arranging an interview.' He lifted his eyes slowly. 'Phil's asked me to take the job. My question is, do you want that, too?'

Jane stared across the desk, her blue eyes meeting his. What was she going to tell him? What could she say? The whole day had been a series of unprecedented events. She could hardly blame Marcus for any of them.

Indeed, it was only with Marcus's help throughout the accident and afterwards, when he had offered to stay and help with the surgeries, that they had managed so well. Both Phil and Cenna had found his presence helpful. She corrected herself. Invaluable. Cenna's postnatal clinic at four had only been possible because Marcus had offered to take the overspill of afternoon patients.

And now he was making the situation clear. If she had reservations about him assuming the role of locum, she must say so now. But how could she? How would she expect Phil to take into consideration what had happened seven years ago? And did she have any right to oppose what must be a sensible—perhaps the *only*—decision for the practice?

Before she could respond a soft knock came at the door and a small figure entered. A large yawn was stifled by the seven-year-old boy who slid comfortably into his father's strong arms.

'Ben, this is Dr Court,' said Marcus, drawing the child against him and ruffling his hair. 'Jane is an old friend of mine from London.'

'Hello, Ben.' Jane smiled even though her veneer of composure was shattered the moment she looked into the child's face. The dark eyes were so like his mother's. Even the boy's hair was a cap of dark silk that fell over his eyes in a wispy wave, like Katrina's.

Ben rubbed his tired eyes and snuggled against his father's shoulder, his gaze cautiously avoiding hers.

'I think it's time we were going, young man,' Marcus whispered against the boy's dark head. Enfolding him against his chest, the black lashes brushed slowly down onto a rosy cheek.

'Had you intended to drive back to London tonight?' Jane asked as Marcus looked up at her.

'That rather depends…' he murmured, his hesitation telling Jane all she needed to know. 'On you.'

Did she really have a choice? she asked herself as she looked into Marcus's questioning gaze. The answer to her silent question was evident and with her next words, she knew that their fate was once again sealed for the foreseeable future.

CHAPTER THREE

THE mixture of minor ailments which had caused the surgery's waiting room to swell had finally abated to a trickle by lunchtime. Jane glanced at her watch, wondering if she dared leave for her calls. The thought struck her, as she lifted the internal phone, that setting out on her rounds before midday would have once been unthinkable. But since Marcus had arrived, all that had changed.

Was it really two weeks since he had walked into the surgery for an interview? Fourteen days and his presence was now as familiar to everyone as any other member of staff's. Marcus himself, though, hadn't attempted to engage her in conversation, yet his attitude was always polite, if distant. They seemed to have fallen into a routine, and to her surprise it had worked.

The crackle of static in her ear brought Jane back to the present as Annie's voice came over the line. 'Cup of coffee before you go, Dr Court?'

'That would be lovely, Annie. And any prescriptions needing a signature.'

'They're all done, thanks to Dr Granger. And he managed two early visits before his clinic, which narrows down the list for you, Dr Court. Three only, and all regulars. Two of the Porchers with flu and Henry Spinney, BP check.'

'Dr Granger took the others?' Jane recalled at least five names listed on the computer screen early that morning.

'Visited them before he arrived. Said he dropped Ben off at school and called on the way to the surgery.' Annie laughed. 'Do you know, I really can't imagine him not being here now. No more early morning panics. We haven't had a breakfast crisis in two weeks. And did you hear that the young man that Marcus treated in the accident came through?'

Jane nodded. 'Yes, Phil told me he had a phone call from Southampton General.'

Jane was well aware of Marcus's attention to the heavy lists that had been building all winter. She was also aware that part of her was reluctant to accept the fact he had so capably fulfilled not only the role of locum but every other member of staff's expectations. One tiny part of her had hoped things might not have gelled so perfectly.

But she had known deep in her heart that doctors like Marcus were rare. He had also been the instrument of good fortune for that young man injured so badly in the car crash. She couldn't deny that she had always known it was total commitment for a man like Marcus, and for one moment the mental picture of them as students returned—James and Marcus and she and Katrina. All four training at the same hospital and all good friends. Katrina, looking up at James with those huge brown trusting eyes, and herself, absorbed with Marcus in a way that first love completely overrode everything, to the extent that even her studies, for a while, had taken second place.

'So you'll have an hour for lunch today, Dr Court,' she heard Annie saying. 'Are you going to take it now or after your visits?'

'Oh, er, after, Annie. I'll grab a sandwich and eat back here.' Jane shook her head a little, as if to clear her mind, and lowered the phone. Staring at her list of calls, she drew a line through those Marcus had completed. Despite Phil's and Cenna's delight at having Marcus at the practice, Jane knew she mustn't allow her preoccupation with the past to affect her work.

As she rose, she acknowledged there was one answer to the problem. Tell Phil and Cenna the whole story. But she had resisted that option and so, too, it appeared, had Marcus. Neither of them, she guessed, wanted to go that way. If she could just keep a sense of proportion about the whole thing, she might just get through this next six months with her pride intact.

And she was honest enough to know that pride was a major factor here. After all, what could she say to Phil and Cenna? 'Marcus and I were engaged, but a friend asked him to marry her because she was pregnant and he agreed. So, that was that.'

Jane glanced at her reflection in the mirror and shook her head. One blonde eyebrow archèd accusingly under a wing of golden hair. 'You know that it wasn't like that,' she told herself sadly.

Oh, yes? So what was it like? demanded her other self.

'Hopeless,' sighed Jane, her voice low. 'Katrina was *dying*... She was desperate for Ben to have a proper father, yet she was still grieving for James...'

Her voice faltered as she met her own gaze. What was she doing, arguing with herself like this? Staring at the pale face and wide blue eyes, she was amazed at her dual conversation. 'There was no one else Katrina could turn to,' she went on, as though listening to someone else. 'We were the only ones...the only ones who could help.'

If only she had been able to reassure Katrina, convince her that she would have done anything—as Marcus would have—to help after James's death. Still desperate with grief for James and devastated by the news of her leukaemia, Katrina had nevertheless made the decision to save her baby, refusing treatment so that Ben could be born. She had been so brave and had suffered such heartache that her desire that Ben should have a proper father had seemed perfectly understandable.

Jane's gaze faltered as she looked away from the mirror. Not that the three of them had reached their decision easily. For each of them it had taken a great deal of soul-searching. But Katrina's concern for her child had touched Marcus deeply. It had been a request that he'd felt compelled to comply with. His own sister had been adopted and their relationship was close. Knowing this, Katrina had felt certain she'd been making the right decision to ask Marcus to care for her baby, and Jane had understood.

'Dr Court?'

Jane spun around, her cheeks filling with hot colour as she saw Annie staring at her across the room.

'Are you all right, Dr Court?' Annie pushed her specs up along her nose, peering at Jane as she moved forward, carrying a pile of records.

'Yes...yes. I'm just leaving, Annie.' To cover her confusion Jane hurried to the cupboard, reaching in for her coat. 'Leave the paperwork on the desk, will you? I'll see to it when I come back.'

'Do you want to take the bleeper with you?' Annie was still staring at her and Jane closed her eyes to compose herself for a brief second before turning. When she did, she smiled levelly at the bewildered receptionist.

'I'd better. Thanks, Annie.' Jane thrust the bleeper into her pocket and reached for her case.

'See you in a little while, then?' Annie's uncertain expression lingered and Jane knew that the only way to reassure her was to make light of the moment.

'Don't worry.' Jane smiled as she turned to go. 'I don't intend to make talking to myself a habit. But if you see me doing it again, just give me a poke in the ribs.'

They parted on laughter, but as Jane climbed into her car she breathed a long sigh. From now on, no more dual conversations in the mirror. Or anywhere else for that matter. She didn't have to explain to anyone, least of all to herself.

As she drove to her first call, dismay swiftly turned to confusion. Marcus had casually entered her life once more. Katrina had died eighteen months after having Ben. If Marcus had wanted to find her, he could have if he'd tried. But he hadn't. And the years had passed and Ben was now seven. So why had she, almost without protest, allowed Marcus into her life again?

He had come to Nair for Ben's sake—not hers. He had offered no explanation as to why he had never sought her out after Katrina's death. And then, almost casually, he had walked into the office...

Jane breathed slowly, trying to concentrate on her driving, ignoring the breath trapped in her lungs, the pain under her ribs. She knew what it was, she understood full well the symptoms her body and mind were manifesting. But there was nothing she could do about them, nothing except pray they would go away.

Heartbreak was untreatable. A sad fact of life, but it was true. She had often considered the manner of some of her patients' ills, especially those older folk who found life unbearable without their partners. Heartbreak was not a medical term, but in her opinion there should be one instituted on its behalf. Somehow she had survived after Marcus had married Katrina, though as the days and months had gone by, heartbreak had eroded her passion for life.

It had taken years to regain that passion—*if* she ever really had. The past was buried and that, she promised herself as she drove through the steep, curving streets of Nair, was where it was going to stay.

All week Jane saw very little of Marcus. She told herself she was doing just fine. That she wasn't going to pieces whenever she saw him. The memories only surfaced when she allowed them to. And no one appeared to notice their avoidance of one another.

A flood of flu patients, the early visitors and several meetings regarding the new premises had all helped to fuel a busy week. On Saturday morning Jane woke, feeling she was...just beginning...to regain control of the cocktail of emotions that had filled her since Marcus had walked into her room on that Tuesday morning.

Jane filled her little kitchen with coffee aroma, putting all thoughts of Marcus from her mind. It was a beautiful April Saturday and she had plans. Without the restriction of either morning duty at the surgery or being on call, the world was her oyster. A walk down by the harbour not two minutes away from her little mews cottage, she decided, or perhaps up onto the cliffs above Nair.

Dressed in dark trousers and a blue angora sweater, Jane flicked open her blind and gazed out onto the cobbled street. Sun danced off every slate roof, the line of semi-detached mews opposite a feast of colour. Blue, yellow, white and pink terraced cottages, with freshly planted window-boxes, they radiated summer.

Hope sprang in her heart and warmed her...though the magic lasted only a few seconds as a metallic silver BMW pulled up to the kerb. Instead of the luxurious balm of reassurance which had seemed attainable when she'd woken that morning, her emotions went into freefall.

Marcus climbed out of the car and walked towards her cottage. He was dressed in a navy-blue sweater and cords, and his dark hair fell over his face, his hand going up to thrust the thick wave back over his head. Jane felt her composure slip away like sand with the tide.

Seconds later, she was opening the door.

'I apologise for bothering you,' he said stiffly, the breeze blowing in his own personal scent as he spoke. 'But I was passing...'

'You'd better come in.' Jane stepped back, then her eyes caught a movement in the car. 'Have you someone with you?'

Marcus nodded, glancing over his shoulder. 'I've got Ben with me, so I won't stop.' He looked back at her, meeting her gaze with a level grey stare. 'It's about your patient, Nancy Farlow. She's asked for a visit this morning. I'm on call and quite happy to see her but, bearing in mind your comments that day in the surgery, I thought you might want to follow it up yourself.'

'What's wrong? Do you know?' Jane asked, somewhat puzzled both by Nancy Farlow's unusual request and the sight of the little boy in the car. She knew that Marcus had found someone to help him with Ben. Why should he be sitting in the car this morning if Marcus was on call?

Marcus shrugged. 'She didn't say. Patty Howard, our Saturday receptionist, took the message but unfortunately didn't get any details. I'm just going in for the records, but I thought it best to check with you first.'

Before Jane could answer, the door of the car opened slightly and Marcus, aware of it, turned and strode away. Jane watched as he opened wide the passenger door and a small, white face looked up at him. Marcus hunkered down to the seat and withdrew something from the interior.

Jane slipped the latch on the door, following Marcus to the car. Looking over his shoulder, her heart squeezed. Dressed in a blue T-shirt and jeans, Ben's small chest rose rapidly as Marcus helped him administer his inhaler.

'It was quite a nasty attack in the middle of the night,' Marcus said quietly, glancing up at Jane. 'I thought we had it under control this morning, but you never can tell.'

'But why didn't you ring me?' Jane protested. 'You can't work if Ben isn't well.'

'There was only the one call.' Marcus shrugged. 'I thought we might manage it.' He ruffled the boy's hair. 'How are you feeling, old chap?'

The little boy's face was very pale but, taking his inhaler from his lips, he nodded. 'Better now.'

It was the brave little smile that caused Jane to say quickly, 'Marcus, this is ridiculous—bring Ben inside into the warm.' She was already holding out her hand, despite Marcus's awkward protests, and with a stab of shock at her response to the warm fingers tightening around hers, she led Ben from the car.

Once inside, they passed under the low-beamed ceiling of her small lounge and into the cosy dinette. Jane helped Ben up on a stool and, opening the fridge, gestured to the jug of freshly prepared juice. 'What would you like to drink, Ben? There's juice, or blackcurrant if you prefer.'

Ben's wide, dark eyes peered into the fridge. 'Blackcurrant, please.'

Jane removed the bottle of cordial just as Marcus followed them into the kitchen. His concerned grey eyes fleetingly met Jane's.

'He'll be fine with me,' she said as Ben gulped down his drink, 'while you make your call.'

'You've no objection to me seeing your patient?'

Jane shook her head slowly. 'The request wasn't specifically for me. It may be that she only has the flu.'

Marcus still looked uneasy. 'But you must have arrangements for the morning?'

'Nothing important. I was just about to have breakfast,' she lied easily, 'so perhaps Ben would like to join me.'

Before his father could reply, Ben nodded and Jane opened a cupboard door, drawing out a packet of crunchy cereal. 'They're my favourite,' the boy said eagerly, still wheezing a little. 'But Mrs Barnes thinks porridge is better.'

Jane glanced at Marcus who grinned, his lips parting into an uncertain smile. 'I'm sure Mrs Barnes is a better judge of breakfast cereal than me, but at weekends we tend to please ourselves.'

'Mrs Barnes is really nice,' Ben volunteered. 'But she's a bit strict sometimes.'

Jane endeavoured to keep a straight face and, looking up at Marcus, their eyes met. 'Well, I think it's unanimous,' she said quickly. 'Breakfast seems to be the order of the day. Don't worry, Ben will be fine with me. I can always ring the surgery and have them bleep you if necessary.'

After Marcus had left, Jane discovered that the little boy,

so disturbingly like his mother in his looks, was nothing like her in character. Katrina had been shy and quiet, her manner often mistaken for aloofness. But Ben was a chatterbox, a lively, outgoing child, despite the tragedy in his young life.

Over breakfast, Ben volunteered the information that Mrs Barnes owned a large and, according to Ben, spooky house, on the clifftops of Nair. The fact that Mrs Barnes obviously doted on her young lodger was evident when Ben related how, during the night, she had heard him coughing and had made him a warm drink as Marcus dealt with the asthma attack.

'Mrs Barnes has three grandchildren, but they all live in America,' Ben explained between small exploratory visits to each corner of her kitchen, dinette and lounge. Resuming his stool and last slice of toast, Ben was swift to declare that Mrs Barnes also played the piano and had a garden where she'd promised, 'in summer we'll have our tea on the lawn.'

After breakfast, Jane showed Ben out into her own small garden. It was no more than a courtyard, but she had filled it with tubs of flowers now beginning to bloom. Garden chairs, a canopied swing seat and a long wooden table perched neatly beside her one concession to luxury, a brick-built barbecue.

Ben ferreted around in the small fish pond, discovering a frog and an army of waterboatmen. Jane brought out bean bags and drinks and they sat amusing themselves in the sunshine. Donovan, Jane's large tabby, made himself comfortable between Ben's legs, and by the time Marcus returned at one, Jane was preparing lunch.

'I'm sorry I'm so late,' he apologised, slightly out of breath as she opened the door. 'We had several more calls after twelve and I thought, as I hadn't heard from you, I would go on to do them. How is Ben?'

'He's feeling much better.'

Marcus looked visibly relieved. 'You were right as regards Nancy Farlow. She has a nasty bout of flu, something she says she hasn't had since she was a teenager. She told me to tell you that because of the flu she cancelled her appointment for the small op, but she hasn't forgotten about coming in.'

Jane nodded. 'I see. Well, it remains to be seen if she does.'

'She sounded genuine enough,' remarked Marcus thoughtfully. Glancing out to the garden, he nodded. 'Now, I'd better relieve you of trouble.'

Jane smiled gesturing to the kitchen. 'I'd hardly call him that. I was just making us some lunch.'

Marcus frowned, his grey eyes moving slowly over her face. 'I think we've made enough of a nuisance of ourselves for one day.'

'Daddy, Daddy, come and look at Donovan,' Ben yelled as he bounced towards them through the French windows. 'He can do tricks, just like a dog.'

'Hey, slow down, young man,' Marcus said, opening his arms to catch his son. 'Now, who is Donovan?'

'Come and see, come and see...' Ben tugged at Marcus's hand. 'He can come to see Donovan, can't he, Dr Court?'

She nodded, barely meeting Marcus's gaze. With a feeling of unreality, she watched Ben lead Marcus through the lounge and into the sunshine. Her eyes felt as though they were looking through a veil, Marcus's tall figure losing its distinction in the sunshine. His dark hair and blue sweater contrasted against the white walls of the garden, his presence seeming to fill it in the same way it had always filled her vision, many years before.

Whenever she'd walked into a room, she'd always sensed Marcus before seeing him. Somehow she'd known he'd be there. Tall and craggy, with a liquid silver gaze that had always linked to hers instantly, she'd never accustomed herself to the sensations which had driven through her as their eyes had met. The same was happening now, beyond her control, the wave of attraction washing through her, filling her up until she forced herself to look away.

Then it was compassion that filled her as her gaze slipped down to the boy who could so easily be mistaken for Marcus's child. A child who would never know his real mother or father. Raven-haired and with Marcus's slightly lopsided smile, what onlooker would ever guess the truth?

Marcus's deep laughter echoed through the French windows as Donovan perched on his back legs, paws swishing the air with feline ingenuity. Jane took in a sharp breath as her senses went into overdrive. The sound of laughter pealing into the house…the sight of Marcus and Ben in her garden…and the scent of summer in the air.

She reached out to steady herself, then made her way slowly to the kitchen. She prepared a light lunch of salad, cheeses and meats, listening to the voices and laughter trickle through from outside. When Ben and Marcus came into the kitchen, their faces were flushed with the fresh air.

'Scrummy,' yelped Ben as he climbed on the stool and watched Jane slice the loaf. 'I love crusty bread. So do you, don't you, Dad?'

'Jane, you really shouldn't have bothered.' Marcus caught her eye. 'I feel we've taken up enough of your time.'

'It's no bother.' Jane placed the salad on the bar. 'Help yourselves. Ben, what would you like for pudding? I've some ice cream in the fridge or there's fruit salad. Or both if you like.'

Ben was already nodding and once again Jane lifted her eyes to Marcus's gaze. There was amusement there, but something more, something shimmering just below the surface of that liquid clarity. Whatever it was it made her shiver. No matter what she told herself about Marcus, the attraction was still there.

After lunch, she made coffee and once more they sat in the garden to drink it. They made conversation, watching

Ben play by the pond. Their talk revolved around Ben and his new school and the indefatigable Mrs Barnes who had made their first few weeks in Nair so comfortable.

Ben's asthma had disappeared completely by the time they left and Jane closed her front door, leaning back on it with a long sigh. She gazed around her house, the sound of Ben's young voice still seeming to echo though the place. Over the last few years she had come to terms with the fact that her life was on course without children or, indeed, marriage.

As for men, she had dated often enough, but no man had ever captured her interest. Trips to the theatre, pleasant meals out and a small circle of good friends, she had settled for these. But there had only ever been one love in her life. All others were a pale and unsatisfactory shadow of the passion she had experienced with Marcus. She was grateful for what she had—a satisfying career, an independent life and good health.

But now, in just a morning, the house had been filled with an intimacy she couldn't begin to describe. Long-forgotten emotions had filled the atmosphere and awoken in her the buried sensations of the past. She felt as though she were in a dream—the child had brought back so much of the time before he was born, when she and Katrina had first met Marcus and James.

She shook herself a little as if trying to clear the memories, but she knew in her heart that something had changed.

The warm weather finally arrived the following week and with it the new influx of temporary residents holidaying in Nair. Jane's own street was home to a number of small guest houses, and as she left for work, people were emerging in shorts, T-shirts and wearing backpacks, a sure sign the season had begun.

Marcus's daily acknowledgement was brief but pleasant,

as was her own. On Tuesday one or two problems had to be resolved regarding the rotas and Jean Thomas, the secretary, approached Jane during her lunch-hour.

'The problem is, Dr Granger will offer to do almost anything,' Jean commented as they sat in the office, poring over the lists for late evenings, visits and on-call duties. 'But I don't want to overload his schedule. He has got his little boy to consider.'

Jane nodded. 'You're right, Jean. And I think we should make his on-call weekend once in every five. I'll do two consecutively—I'm quite happy with that. Cenna and Phil will go along with one each per month.'

'Are you sure?' Jean asked her apprehensively. 'Are you still happy to have Thursdays off?'

'Yes, no problem.'

'Well, that helps a lot.' Jean sighed contentedly, marking off the dates with a flourish. 'We've no clinics running on Thursday, so it's usually quite reasonable in surgery. Thanks, Jane, I'll print these out for everyone now.'

As Jane went on to her surgery she wondered what Marcus did with his weekends when he wasn't on call. There was Ben to occupy, of course, and now the weather was better they probably enjoyed the harbour and the sandy coves of Nair to their fullest. She wondered if the boy's asthma had shown any improvement and whether or not Nair was having the desired effect that Marcus had hoped it would.

It was a surprise therefore when on Friday, just as she was leaving surgery, Ben ran towards her, his little face wreathed in smiles. 'Dr Court, Dr Court, how's Donovan?' He landed in Jane's arms as she reached out to steady him his fingers wrapped tightly around hers.

'He's fine, Ben. But what are you doing here?'

'The bus driver dropped me off.'

Jane looked up to see the school bus juddering noisily

at the kerb. The driver had his thumb raised and she nodded, waving her approval.

'He has to make sure someone meets me,' Ben explained
breathlessly. ''Cos usually I stay with Mrs Barnes till Dad
gets home.'

'Why aren't you going home to Mrs Barnes today?'

'She's gone to Dorchester to see her daughter. So Dad
rang the school and said that I had to be dropped off at the
surgery.'

'I see.' Jane looked down at the tiny figure in a rather
large navy blue blazer, his hand clasped firmly around hers.
'Would you like me to walk into the surgery with you?'

Ben nodded, his large brown eyes fringed by dark lashes.
He was so like Katrina, Jane thought as another little shock
passed through her.

'Are you going home now?' the boy asked her as they
walked towards the door.

'Yes, I'm just on my way.'

'How's Donovan?' The mumbled question came as they
stopped, making way for a patient to enter ahead of them.

'Oh, he's fine.' Jane's deep blue eyes met Ben's wide
brown ones and she found herself unable to resist the question written plainly in them. 'If your father agrees, would
you like to come with me and see him?'

Ben nodded eagerly. *'Yes, please.'*

Jane smiled and squeezed the small hand entwined in
hers. 'Well, if he's not busy with a patient, you could pop
into his room. I'll wait for you at Reception.'

But Paula explained that Marcus's patient had just gone
in and Ben's face fell. 'Your father will be some while,
Ben,' she said regretfully. 'The appointment is a double
one, I'm afraid. But I could give him a message. I'm sure
he would rather you were with Dr Court than sitting in the
office, watching TV.'

Though Jane was uncertain about this, Ben's eager response made it impossible for her to refuse, and a few

minutes later they were outside once more and climbing into her car. On the drive home, Ben chatted non-stop about school and the new friends he'd made. When they arrived at the cottage Donovan was sitting on the front step, preening. Ben climbed out of the car eagerly to stroke him.

'Are you hungry?' Jane asked as she unlocked her front door.

'Mmm. Ever so,' Ben replied enthusiastically as he scooped the purring Donovan into his arms.

'I'll make some tea,' Jane suggested as she called to mind what supplies she had hidden in the freezer. 'How about fish fingers and beans?'

'I love fish fingers' was the eager response, before a pair of large brown eyes swivelled towards the French windows and the garden. 'Can we go and play by the pond, Dr Court?'

'I don't see why not.' Jane shrugged as she took off her coat and filled the kettle with water. 'Hang your blazer and schoolbag in the hall cupboard first.'

For a moment she glanced round as the little figure, cat in arms, trotted obediently off to the hall. After making herself a cup of tea, Jane glanced out to the garden. Ben and Donovan sat together by the pond, the early evening sun lighting up the little courtyard with soft, warm rays, and for a second or two her heart beat faster.

CHAPTER FOUR

MARCUS arrived at six-thirty that evening. 'I hope Ben didn't inflict himself on you' was his first—apologetic—remark as he stood on the doorstep. 'Paula said he was rather eager to whisk you away.'

Inviting him in, Jane made it clear that it had been entirely her idea to spirit Ben home for tea. 'I was leaving the surgery when the bus dropped him off,' she added as they walked through to the lounge. 'And I was coming straight home tonight, anyway.'

'Well, all I can say, again, is thank you.' Marcus was wearing a white shirt and grey tie and dark trousers, and his skin already had the grainy texture of a tan. Against the pure white of the shirt, the deep honey was a stark contrast. His thick black hair swept back from his face. It had grown longer than she recalled him ever wearing it.

'Would you like coffee?' she asked uncertainly.

He shook his head, his gaze travelling out through the French windows to the garden where Ben was playing. 'I'd better get back. Mrs Barnes is doing something special for supper tonight—it's her daughter's birthday and somehow I got persuaded into a family gathering.'

Jane smiled. 'You seem to have made an impact with Mrs Barnes. Ben has been telling me all about her.'

Marcus lifted his eyes. 'No doubt. She's really a very sweet lady, but sometimes she tends to forget that Ben and I have been on our own for years and don't need to be fussed over.'

It was said casually, and as Marcus met her gaze Jane felt there was more to the remark than she had at first realised. Just then Ben came running in through the lounge, his cheeks rosy from the fresh air.

'Dad, you should see Donovan,' he burst out excitedly. 'He tried to catch the fish with his paw, but he can't 'cos there's some netting over the pond and—'

'I'm sure he's a very clever cat,' Marcus interrupted, gently laying a hand on his son's shoulder. 'But now it's time to go. Fetch your blazer and make sure you've tidied away.'

'Oh, Dad, do we have to leave?' Ben protested, his face dropping.

'We do,' Marcus said firmly, ruffling the boy's mop of dark hair. 'Hurry up now. And, Ben, have you thanked Dr Court for giving up her valuable time for you?'

Ben looked up at Jane with big brown eyes. 'Thank you for having me, Dr Court.'

'It was fun, Ben.' She gave him a smile and nodded to the hall. 'Run and find your blazer and bag now.'

When he had disappeared, Jane glanced up at Marcus. 'He's a lovely child. You must be very proud of him.'

Marcus nodded, his broad shoulders lifting under the crisp white linen. 'Yes...I am. I think his mother would have been, too.'

Jane recognised the change in Marcus's tone as he spoke of Katrina, and her eyes met his searchingly, but before either of them could speak again Ben came running in and the moment had passed. When they left, she waved to Ben as the metallic silver BMW disappeared up the hill, his small face smiling from the back window.

It was a beautiful evening and the sky lay like candyfloss over the rooftops, dipping into the hollows, splashing the horizon. As she returned to the kitchen and began clearing the dishes, she wondered what Marcus would have gone on to say had there been time.

Katrina would, without doubt, have been proud of Ben,

and for a moment Jane felt a wave of sadness sweep over her that she'd not been part of Ben's upbringing, too. Despite the fact she had made a new life for herself after leaving London, forging a close circle of friends, she had never failed to treasure the memory of those early years when they had all been young and good friends.

When James had died, she had tried so hard to support Katrina during the discovery of her pregnancy and the leukaemia…no one had known how long Katrina would survive without treatment. And when Marcus had married Katrina, he had done so knowing that she, Jane, had wished only to support them both.

Then where had it begun to go wrong? Jane's mind was once again revolving over the same old questions as she stood there, slowly placing the cups and saucers on the table. When had Katrina come to distance herself and why? Jane could only assume that Katrina's insecurities after her marriage to Marcus had deepened, and Jane had had no wish to pose a threat to the friend who had already suffered so much.

Suddenly Jane jumped, jolted from her thoughts by Donovan who had leapt onto the worktop and buried his face against her arm. His purr vibrated through her skin and she picked him up and lowered him to the floor, gently stroking his head. The sight of him rolling on his back caused her to smile as she remembered Ben, and his delight in the cat's company.

A small pang went through her as she realised just how much she had enjoyed being with Ben. And this was followed by the inevitable maternal ache which had never been satisfied. She had longed for a family over the years— but there had only been one man in her life. And he had married another woman…

Jane turned back to the window and gazed out on the glorious evening. As much as she was drawn to Ben, she had to maintain a distance between them. It would be utterly foolish to allow herself to become fond of him. In another six months or so Marcus would be moving on, a fact that she herself had taken pains to point out.

The following week, Nair was warmed by a soft southerly wind and the skies were blue and cloudless. A dazzling sun crept higher each day and fishermen cast their nets, dropping pots overboard for the lobsters. Trawlers at sea cast deeper and longer into the day. The first enthusiastic visitors spread out their towels on the deserted beaches.

On Wednesday Jane's surgery was packed, and amongst her patients were Sue Porcher and her little girl, Natasha. 'I never thought I'd see the end of my child-bearing days,' Sue told Jane as she lay on the couch. 'I always think, just one more—and that's it. I couldn't have some other treatment for the fibroids, could I, Dr Court? Is a hysterectomy really necessary?'

Jane pressed gently around Sue's abdomen. 'Well, your consultant seems to think so, Sue, and I have to say I agree with him. Fibroids are non-cancerous tumours, but they're causing you a great deal of pain. I really can't see another alternative.'

Her patient gave a long sigh. 'I know some people think six kids is a bit much, but I wanted a boy for Brian.'

'Don't you find you have enough though to cope with?' Jane asked as she patted Sue's stomach and gestured for her to sit up. 'When do you and Brian ever get time for yourselves? He's fishing all day and sometimes at night. Goodness knows where you squeeze in time for each other.'

'We don't, frankly,' said Sue, sitting up and pulling on her clothes. 'And that's the frightening part. You get into a habit of orbiting around the place, missing each other by minutes, sometimes not even seeing each other for a couple of days.'

'Well, don't you think you owe it to yourselves to ease up a little on the family stakes? You could look at this as a bonus. In a sense, the decision is taken out of your hands. With no babies to look after you might start seeing a lot more of one another.'

Sue gave an ironic chuckle. 'Perhaps that's what I'm afraid of, Dr Court.'

Jane smiled softly. 'No, you're not. I know you, Sue. You worship that man of yours.'

The still attractive mother of six nodded slowly. 'Yes, we've had our moments, I suppose.' She glanced up and grinned at Jane. 'Well, about six to be precise.'

Both women burst into laughter, despite the subject of Sue Porcher's looming hysterectomy. Eventually Sue wheeled two-year-old Natasha, asleep in the pushchair, back to Jane's desk. 'What exactly do they remove in a hysterectomy?' she asked as Jane wrote out a prescription for pain relief.

Jane looked up, noting the apprehension in her patient's troubled eyes. 'Mr Lucas has made no mention of removing your ovaries,' Jane told her patient, 'so the surgical removal will be of the uterus and cervix. You may have an abdominal incision or it may be done through the vagina, but I suspect the former.'

'And what are the after-effects?' Sue asked hesitantly.

'Provided at least one ovary remains, you shouldn't have any hormone-related problems. A natural menopause may occur a little earlier but, then, it might not.'

Sue flushed slightly. 'And what about…you know, our love-making? I've heard that a hysterectomy really puts some women off sex.'

Jane shook her head. 'Don't listen to old wives' tales, Sue. The vagina and other genital organs aren't affected by a hysterectomy. A woman's sexual activity isn't impaired and your sexual desire shouldn't change.'

At this Sue looked at Jane and grinned. 'I can tell Brian that on your authority, can I?'

The light-hearted remark again brought more laughter until finally Sue rose to her feet, glancing down at her sleeping child. 'Oh, well, I suppose it's all for the best, but I don't know what I'm going to do when I get broody.'

'You might not,' Jane said lightly as she walked to the door. 'You might enjoy the benefits and surprise yourself.'

'I might,' said Sue, and laughed as she left.

Jane closed the door and went back to her desk, reflecting on Sue and Brian's relationship. Their marriage was solid, but Sue deserved to take a rest. She really had worked hard with her family and, as Natasha was the only child not at school, Sue's life should change for the better.

Jane glanced at the computer screen and saw that her next patient was Nancy Farlow, but it was a changed woman who walked into her consulting room. She looked tired and anxious and for the first time ever appeared without her make-up. 'I've been made redundant,' she told Jane as she sat down, pulling an ancient sweater around her. 'It was after my bout of flu. I went back and they told me the firm was winding down. I couldn't believe it.'

'I'm sorry to hear that.' Jane frowned. 'Didn't you have any idea of what was happening?'

'Well, there are always rumours going round a big concern like the one I worked for.' Her patient shrugged, passing a weary hand across her forehead. 'But I usually ignore them. I'll have been with Megga Marketing fifteen years next month. Management say they are putting together a package for the redundancies, but it's not so much the money as thinking how much of my life I've put into that place.'

'You'll find somewhere else, I'm sure,' Jane said

quickly. 'With your qualifications and experience, you'll
have no trouble. And in the meantime we can get your
health sorted out.'

For the first time, Nancy smiled. 'Yes, there is that to it,
I suppose. I really don't have any excuse now, do I, Dr
Court?' She began to remove her sweater. 'I'm afraid the
mole under my bra is rather irritating. I seemed to have
scratched it again.'

On examination of her patient Jane saw that the mole
had changed in size and texture, and she decided without
hesitation to remove them. 'I'd also like you to see an oph-
thalmologist,' she explained as she looked more closely at
her patient's face. 'You have a small area here…just under
your eye…that I would like an opinion on.'

'My eye!' Nancy Farlow's hand went up to her face. 'But
it's just a small blemish, isn't it?'

'I'd like a second opinion,' Jane explained. 'The eye is
a very delicate area and requires special attention.'

'But why is this happening? Is it stress, or is it a skin
disease of some sort?' Nancy Farlow looked shocked as
she sat down at Jane's desk.

'Let's not jump to too many conclusions before removing these,' Jane said as she lifted the internal phone. 'Paula
will arrange an initial appointment for you on Friday. After
that we'll know more.'

When Nancy Farlow left, Jane considered her patient's
skin problems. Nancy had a point—the blemishes could be
a stressful reaction to her current circumstances. But Jane
was almost certain the diagnosis would prove to be skin
cancer. Nancy's exposure to sunlight or ultraviolet radiation
during her stay in Australia might have been the cause,
though other factors included a genetic predisposition,
light-coloured skin, blue or green eyes, blond or red hair.
Perhaps Nancy's blue eyes and blonde hair were a strong
family trait. However, nothing could be done until the re-

sults were returned and she discussed the outcome with her patient.

It was half past six before she finished that evening and she felt restless. Deciding the weather was warm enough for her first swim of the year, Jane returned to her cottage and changed into shorts and a T-shirt. Pushing her bathing costume and towel into a beach bag, she headed for the sea. Tomorrow, Thursday, was her day off, so there was no need for an early night. She could bathe, eat late and relax without rushing.

Her chosen spot was north of Nair, an arc of white sandy beach that was known to the locals. A long and winding cliff path was the only safe route when the tide was in, and access to the beach was slow.

Parking her car at the top of the cliffs, Jane made her way down the narrow path. The breeze was a gentle ripple against her face and lifted her blonde hair softly across her cheeks. She felt a stir of excitement inside as the white-crested waves sparkled like gems under the glowing sunset.

At the bottom of the path, Jane paused to watch the dwindling handful of sunbathers. One woman in a swimsuit strode across the beach towards the sea. An older woman accompanied her, a plump lady who hitched up her skirt to paddle.

For a moment Jane smiled at the scene, watching the women talking leisurely on the sand. Suddenly a boy appeared from a hole in the sand where he had been digging. Jane's heart missed a beat as she recognised him, his skinny little legs carrying him towards the water.

'Time to go home now, Ben,' warned the older woman, her voice carrying on the breeze.

Jane's eyes followed the progress of the three figures as they began to walk slowly across the sand. Ben trailed behind the two women, jumping the waves and splashing in the surf. His small frame and dark hair were so much like his mother's that Jane watched them until finally they disappeared from sight. Katrina's presence, for one moment, seemed to hang in the air, and slowly Jane turned, retracing her steps up the cliff path, the swim that she had so longed for suddenly devoid of appeal.

Jane did very little the following day, meeting her friends at the gym and playing their weekly game of squash. She promised herself that part of the evening she would spend in the garden, but by the time she'd brought home the shopping and settled down for some supper, the sun had dipped below the wall of the courtyard.

That night, sleep didn't come easily. She thought about Ben and his small figure dancing along the water's edge the previous day and how the memories of Katrina and the past had flooded back into her mind. She hadn't been prepared for the mixture of emotions which had overwhelmed her. Perhaps it had just been catching sight of him so unexpectedly that had brought everything back. Or perhaps she was being ridiculously sentimental.

Feeling annoyed with herself for indulging in a kind of self-torture, Jane sat up, switched on the bedside lamp and tried to read. But even when her eyes were closing and she lay down again to sleep, her mind still persisted in its tireless activity.

And so it was the following morning that she welcomed Annie's warning of a busy day. The last thing she wanted was time on her hands. She wanted to shake off the strange mood that seemed to oppress her, and she knew from experience that work was the cure.

Nancy Farlow's appointment was booked for afternoon surgery and Jane prepared for the small op in the treatment room. Gaynor Botterill, the practice nurse, prepared the trolley, and when Nancy arrived Jane wasted no time in applying a local anaesthetic, excising the two areas of concern and tying off six neat sutures over each small wound.

'That was over quicker than I thought,' remarked Nancy as she tucked in her shirt and gave a sigh of relief. 'When do you think the results will be back?'

'Hopefully in a week or so,' Jane replied as she washed her hands and dried them. 'Meanwhile your hospital appointment will come through.'

Nancy Farlow nodded. 'I'm going for a couple of interviews early next week so I'll ring in on Friday.'

'That was quick work,' Jane said in surprise.

'Oh, they aren't jobs that challenge me much, unfortunately, but I just can't bear the thought of being unemployed. I feel totally lost.'

'But why?' Jane probed gently. 'You deserve to have a break and if, as you said, finances aren't a problem...'

'All I know is,' said her patient, holding up her hand, 'that moping around at home leaves me totally unfulfilled. I need to be working. And if I don't find myself a job, Dr Court, you'll find me back here demanding some antidepressants or some such dreadful stuff.'

'I'm sure it won't come to that,' Jane returned with a wry smile. 'Though once in a while many people feel the need for a little extra support in their lives and consider either medication or therapy.' She frowned curiously at her patient. 'Tell me, what happens when you do finally stop work?'

'You mean...*retirement*?' Nancy Farlow gasped in mock surprise. 'Look, Dr Court, I'll find something to keep me busy. I mean, I just can't imagine myself as the little woman at home, washing and ironing. I'm just not cut out for that way of life.'

When Jane was on her own once more she thought—not for the first time—how diverse her patients were. It was the Sue Porchers and Nancy Farlows of the world, as dif-

ferent as chalk to cheese, who made her job so interesting.
She'd thought when she'd first come to Nair after her year's
training with a London practice, that life might be dull at
a seaside resort. But there hadn't been a day when something hadn't captured her interest. And though her life had
seemed empty without Marcus, Nair had slowly brought
the colour back into her life.

Just then a knock came at the door and, expecting to see
her next patient, she was surprised to see Phil. She beckoned him in, noticing that he looked unusually smart in a
dark suit and tie. He was a handsome man in every respect,
his features strong and cleanly cut, his smile wide and
friendly. But since Maggie's accident he'd had an anxious
look that had clouded his brown eyes and etched worry
lines across his forehead. At thirty-eight, Jane knew her
partner was still struggling to come to terms with his wife's
untimely death.

'Just wondered what you thought of an idea...a staff
meeting in a week's time?'

Jane shrugged. 'Certainly. To discuss anything special,
Phil?'

He pulled out the chair and sat down, a wry expression
on his face. 'Yes, pretty special, actually.' His smile broad-
ened and he gave a quiet laugh. 'The last part of the extension on the new practice has just been given the go-
ahead.'

Jane rose to her feet. 'Oh, Phil, that's wonderful news.'

'Yes, it is, isn't it?'

She was soon at his side and bent to hug him. 'Con-
gratulations, you've worked so hard for this, Phil.'

'Well, we all have,' he said modestly, squeezing her
hand.

'Does this mean we're back on schedule for the new
practice?'

He nodded as he looked up at her. 'With a little luck,

yes. I went to have a look round last night with a chap from the borough surveyor's department. There seems to be nothing unduly to worry about, so I thought I'd just fill everyone in, now that I have something definite.'

'When do you think the completion date will be? By the end of autumn, as hoped?'

Her partner nodded. 'Well, hopefully, if all goes well.'

'It's been tough for you, Phil.' Jane sighed as she perched on the edge of her desk. 'But the new place will be worth it.'

He grinned. 'Certainly hope so. Anyway, Cenna suggested we have a celebratory meeting—a party, really. She offered to host it at her house. I suggested we have it here but she said she'd like to use the opportunity for a house-warming since she's only just moved.'

'What a wonderful idea,' Jane said quickly. 'I'll see what I can do to help. I'll have a chat with her later.'

'Great.' Phil frowned then and, rising to his feet, glanced over his shoulder. 'I think it's only fair to ask Marcus. He isn't involved, I know, though I have to say, if he showed the least bit of interest, I'd be in there like a shot. But I understand he has other things planned for next year, so I guess that's it.'

'Have you asked him about staying on?' Jane tried not to reveal the shock in her voice.

'No, just hinted really. He'd be a good man to have. But as soon as I broach the subject, he makes it plain he doesn't want to know. Whatever it is he's got planned, it's obviously something important to him.'

'I see,' Jane murmured hesitantly. 'Well, I'm sure we'll find someone when we advertise later in the year. The new premises will be a very attractive proposition for anyone interested in a partnership.'

Phil gave a small shrug as he stood uneasily by the door.

'Yes, I hope so. But I thought…well…since you seemed to be getting on rather well with young Ben…'

'What do you mean?' Jane flushed as she stood there. 'You aren't asking *me* to try to persuade Marcus to stay in Nair, I hope?'

'Oh, no…no,' Phil replied uncertainly, looking at her with disappointment written all over his face. 'I just thought…well, I just wondered if you offered to take him down to the new site and show him around…'

'Phil, nothing I have to say will influence Marcus,' Jane protested. She couldn't believe Phil was suggesting this. But, then, she reminded herself, Phil knew nothing of their history and had no idea how she felt about Marcus working at the practice.

'I suppose,' murmured Phil dejectedly, 'I'm clutching at straws. I just know he'd make a good partner—good for us and for Nair. You must admit, he's absolutely right for the place. And if Ben's asthma is helped by the coastal environment…' He stopped, her obvious disinterest causing him to shrug and with a soft sigh open the door. 'Well, it was worth a try,' he said ruefully. 'Anyway, you're on for a week on Saturday, right?'

She nodded. 'I'll be there.'

He grinned and winked, nevertheless leaving her with the feeling that she'd gone out of her way to be unhelpful. She sank down on her seat and lowered her head into her hands. The irony of it was that Phil was right. It was clear that Marcus would have made the perfect partner for the new surgery.

Cenna watched from her car as her two colleagues, Jane Court and Marcus Granger, passed by one another and headed in different directions. Marcus entered the surgery, while Jane, seeing Cenna's blue Toyota, waved and hurried across the car park.

'Am I late?' she asked breathlessly as she climbed in beside Cenna. 'Sorry. I had one late arrival. Have we time for lunch?'

Cenna glanced at her watch. 'Three quarters of an hour. That will do.' She started the engine and drove the car out of the car park and down the hill into Nair.

'Fisherman's Haunt OK?' she asked as she drove past the quay.

'Oh, lovely.' Jane smiled as she nodded to the narrow road that would lead them to the quiet harbour cul-de-sac. 'I love their prawn sandwiches and I'm gasping for a long, cool drink.'

Cenna enjoyed her occasional lunch with Jane. Since coming to Nair three years ago, Cenna had known that she and Jane would be good friends and she hadn't been proven wrong. What Cenna found difficult to understand was that such an attractive woman like Jane was still unattached. They both belonged to the squash club and the gym and often exercised together and had mutual friends but, despite Jane's gregarious nature, she had never dated anyone for very long.

But Cenna had sensed rather than observed some flash of chemistry between Jane and Marcus. Neither Jane or Marcus had given the impression of knowing one another, but Cenna was curious. Their body language, their glances, even their indifference towards each other had set her thinking.

As they walked into the quaint old inn, Cenna nodded to the window table they liked to sit at. Luckily, the table was free and giving their orders at the bar, Cenna joined Jane to look out over the harbour.

A turquoise sky and white fluffy clouds made up the view she knew so well. Small fishing craft dotted the water, fishermen sat on the harbour walls and chatted to the visitors. A fresh fish stall was keenly patronised by a number of women, almost certainly owners of hotels, and a conservation kiosk was setting up shop for the local bird-life.

'It's beautiful, isn't it?' sighed Jane, looking cool and summery in a calf-length cream frock and thin navy belt. Her blonde hair was swept up in a bunch on top of her head with a large tortoiseshell clip and her fringe fell softly over her forehead.

Cenna nodded, brushing back her thick dark hair with her hand, her beautiful amber eyes surveying the scene. She felt cool and relaxed in her pale blue shirt and trousers. Wednesday was usually her day off, but this week she was taking Friday in order to prepare for Saturday's get-together.

'Now, how can I help on Saturday?' Jane asked as a young girl brought them a large plate of fresh prawn sandwiches and two tall glasses of sparkling mineral water.

'I'm doing a buffet,' Cenna explained. 'Quiches, salads, crusty bread, cheese and pickles. Anything you can add to that will be very welcome.'

'What if I bring trifles and fresh cream—and one or two other desserts?' Jane suggested as they ate.

Cenna nodded, licking her lips. 'Wonderful. I think Phil's ordering the drinks. He said he was organising the numbers over the next few days.'

Jane laughed. 'This sounds like a real celebration.'

'Well it is in a way, isn't it?' Cenna grinned. 'After all, one way or another, now that the extension is approved, we're almost there.' She took a sidelong glance at Jane. 'It's just a pity Marcus won't be coming with us,' she said quietly, and met Jane's eyes.

'What do you mean?' Jane frowned at Cenna over the rim of her glass.

Cenna opened her amber eyes wide. 'Well, he is the obvious choice for a new partner, isn't he?'

'Phil seems to think so, too,' Jane answered, staring down at the drink in her hands.

Cenna took a bite of prawn sandwich and slowly licked her lips. 'Jane…would you mind if I asked you something?'

Her friend sat back, her blue eyes regarding Cenna with uncertainty. 'It's about Marcus, isn't it?'

Cenna nodded. 'Tell me to mind my own business if you like, but have you two met before?'

Jane looked out of the window, her white teeth trapping her bottom lip for one moment. Then she turned back and met Cenna's gaze. 'What gave us away?' she asked quietly.

'So you and Marcus *do* know one another?' Cenna said on a little gasp.

Jane nodded slowly. 'Yes, we do. Is it that obvious?'

Cenna shrugged. 'No, not at all. I guess it's just my woman's intuition that there was something between you.'

'Cenna if you've noticed that, I'm sure others have, too. Has Phil said anything to you?'

'Nothing at all. And I'm sure no one else knows.'

Jane was silent until finally she sighed. 'Marcus and I trained together in London,' she said slowly. 'He was two years ahead of me but we met at a hospital party…and fell in love. We planned to get engaged when he qualified, but…but things went wrong. Terribly wrong. Marcus married someone else.'

'Oh, Jane—I'm sorry.'

Jane shook her head slowly. 'It's all history now, of course. But, you see, I had no idea Marcus would apply for the job and it was a shock when he arrived.'

'It must have been. Did he know you were working in Nair?'

'Phil told him when he applied for the job, but by then it was too late. Marcus thought if I had any objections to his interview I would raise them and he wouldn't attend.'

'But Phil forgot and Marcus arrived on the day of the accident?'

'Yes.' Jane looked up. 'It was a dreadful mix-up.'

'I realise now why you said so little,' Cenna murmured, recalling Jane's strange behaviour on that day. But somehow she had known Marcus and Jane were connected. She really couldn't say how, only that it was a gut feeling, a sense of intimacy that denied the coolness between them. And there was that expression in Marcus's eyes whenever he looked at Jane and the disguised emotion that lay trapped in Jane's blue eyes.

'Love hurts, doesn't it?' Cenna answered quietly. 'No matter what you tell yourself, it really does hurt. You must have been devastated when Marcus got married to someone else.'

'When I look back it sounds unbelievable,' Jane replied as she lifted her drink and sipped it. Replacing it on the table, she met Cenna's gaze. 'There were four of us, Marcus and I, my friend Katrina and James Conway. We met the boys in our first year and I suppose you could say it was love at first sight. James was Katrina's first and only romance. She adored him. They were inseparable, and when James was killed in a road traffic accident Katrina was devastated. She never really recovered from the shock. So when she found out she was pregnant, Marcus and I did everything we could to help her.'

'And it was Katrina who Marcus married?'

'Yes, but it wasn't like that, Cenna.' Jane hesitated. 'You see, during Katrina's pregnancy it was discovered she had leukaemia. She refused treatment because of the baby. There was no one else to help her, except us—Marcus and I. She wanted James's baby more than anything else…'

'And Ben is James's baby, not Marcus's son?' Cenna guessed.

Jane nodded. 'The prognosis was bad for Katrina. We

knew she hadn't long to live without treatment. We didn't even know if she would survive the pregnancy. But she did, and there was one thing she asked of us...and...and we agreed.' Jane's voice shook slightly. 'She asked Marcus to marry her for the child's sake, knowing that if anything happened to her the baby would be cared for.'

'Assuming you agreed? Because you would eventually have become Ben's stepmother?'

Jane nodded. 'How could we refuse?'

Cenna watched her friend's face sadden and saw the grief clearly written in her eyes. 'Oh, Jane, what a sacrifice for you. What about Katrina's parents? Wouldn't they help?'

Jane looked down at the table and shook her head. 'No. They didn't want anything to do with the baby. Cenna, she was dying and she was alone. It was so heartbreaking.'

'So Marcus married Katrina and took Ben on as his own?'

'Yes. But...but I left London before Katrina died...eighteen months later.'

'But why—wasn't it part of the arrangement for you to stay?'

Jane lowered her head, her voice low. 'It was, yes. But Katrina seemed to change, become less friendly. Marcus qualified and joined a small group practice...and Ben was a lovely, healthy baby. I...I can only assume Katrina felt threatened in some way, and when I realised she didn't want me to visit, I—I...' Jane stopped, unable to continue.

'Oh, Jane, what a terrible situation. How did you cope?'

Jane lifted her shoulders and looked up at Cenna. 'I decided to leave London and went abroad as soon as I qualified. I couldn't stay knowing that was how Katrina felt—she deserved whatever happiness she could find...' Jane's voice broke as she put her hand to her mouth.

'I'm so sorry, Jane,' Cenna said softly. 'It seems so unfair. How sad for all of you.'

Jane nodded. 'But that's life, isn't it?'

'Didn't Marcus contact you after Katrina's death?'

Jane shook her head slowly, fighting back the emotion. 'No. I took it that he didn't want to. Perhaps…perhaps…'

'You think he might have fallen in love with Katrina?' Cenna interrupted in a shocked voice.

Jane trapped her bottom lip with her teeth, her eyes telling Cenna how much that painful truth had haunted her. Clearing her throat, she said quietly, 'I'm going to explain the situation to Phil eventually, but for the moment I'd appreciate it if you keep what I've told you between us.'

Cenna nodded. 'Of course.'

Nair Surgery had had its fair share of tragic stories, Cenna reflected sadly. There was Paula Locke, whose fisherman husband had been drowned at sea two years ago, and Phil, of course. Maggie Jardine had, like Katrina, died achingly young. He must have been heartbroken and yet he had never allowed himself the luxury of self-pity. In the months since Maggie's death, Phil had thrown himself into work. And she worried about him…

Cenna looked up, aware that Jane was frowning at her. She just hoped that her friend wasn't able to guess her thoughts…

CHAPTER FIVE

SATURDAY arrived with a full list of morning patients. Jane noted the increase in holidaymakers staying at the small guest houses in her street and wondered how many would be signing on at the surgery during the course of their holiday.

Her answer came by way of assorted ills arriving in the form of temporary residents at the surgery that morning. Coughs, colds and sore throats were numerous. By midday she was finally finished and left Patty Howard, the Saturday morning receptionist, to lock up.

Nair shopping centre was her first stop before returning home. Jane intended to make the desserts she had promised Cenna, before spoiling herself with a hairdo. Her long blonde hair was in desperate need of a trim and when she arrived home, after shopping, she rang the hairdresser's and made an appointment.

The afternoon went fairly smoothly, but as she placed the trifles in the fridge to set the telephone rang. 'Jane, I wonder if I could ask a favour?' Phil said hurriedly. 'I'm on call this afternoon, as you know. Is there any chance you could drop by Marcus's place? I gave him all the paperwork on the new practice—everything right back from the germination of the idea, three years ago. I forgot to ask him for it last night and I'd like to have it for this evening, should anyone be interested.'

Jane glanced at her watch. 'Phil, I'm just off to the hairdresser's—why not ring Marcus and ask him to bring it to you?'

'I have done, but his landlady says he's out for the afternoon. And as you only live ten minutes away, I thought you wouldn't mind stopping by on your way over tonight.'

Jane paused. 'OK, Phil, but I feel rather awkward.'

'You mean because Marcus isn't involved in the new place?'

'Yes...'

'Well, it isn't for the want of asking, I can assure you,' Phil interrupted briskly. 'I've tried my darnedest to persuade him into coming tonight.'

'You have?'

'Oh, yes. But he gave some excuse about decorating. Frankly, Jane, I've a feeling he thinks I've been trying to oversell the new practice a bit.'

'I see.' Jane felt she couldn't refuse. 'Well, all right, then. I'll ring Cenna and tell her I might be a little late.'

'I'm in your debt,' Phil replied gratefully. 'The bleeper and phone have been going non-stop so far. I've a locum organised to take over for later in the evening so I hope to make it to Cenna's in time.'

When Jane replaced the phone, she wished she'd thought up some excuse not to call on Marcus. Normally, she wouldn't have minded running an errand for Phil, no matter what it was. But in this instance it was difficult, though, of course, Phil didn't realise the implications of his request.

And just what were the implications? Jane asked herself as she hurriedly got ready for the hairdresser. Would Marcus think she had deliberately made herself available to call? And if so, what would he think her reasons were?

Endeavouring to put the thought behind her, Jane made her way to the hairdresser's, a small salon she used in the town centre. When she left there, a loud thunderclap rumbled above and the heavens opened. Nair high street suddenly emptied of visitors. The little gift shops and cafés were closed, and by the time Jane had made a dash back to the car her new hairdo was soaked. The silky blonde bob that her hairdresser had crafted so smoothly around her face suddenly turned into a cap of damp fronds.

Jane wondered if the day was going to turn out a complete disaster. On the spur of the moment, she stopped her car outside the boutique in which she had bought her last dress well before Christmas. To her surprise the shop assistant was still busy with customers.

Studying her reflection in the driving mirror, Jane saw the raindrops clinging to her newly styled fringe and two large black panda eyes staring back at her. The dismal sight caused her to switch off the engine, and pull her jacket up to her ears and leap from the car.

Rain streamed in the gutters, another loud thunderburst crashed overhead and Jane found herself sheltering in the doorway, staring at a dress in the window. How a little black number like that cost the absolute earth, she had no idea. It certainly wasn't her cup of tea—far too short, far too skimpy.

But a quarter of an hour later she was on her way home with windscreen washers rapping wildly at the windscreen, the dress beside her, wrapped in a designer label bag.

'You're crazy,' Jane muttered to herself an hour later as she drove towards the Westcliffe area of Nair. 'Absolutely crazy. Why buy something so expensive for a staff party?'

'Well, why not?' she muttered back, accelerating up the steep hill. 'You haven't bought yourself anything new in months. You deserve something that's fun and—and totally inappropriate for the evening.'

Jane shook her head a little, frowning out into the damp spring night. 'At least it's stopped raining,' she sighed, appreciating the perfumed scents drifting in through her open window. She really had to stop talking to herself like this—the next thing she would be doing would be holding a full discussion and interrupting herself!

Mrs Barnes's large house was to be found on the top of the cliff, Jane knew that. Ben had given her directions when describing the 'creepy old house' that he was sure had a spook of some sort.

Jane smiled to herself, recalling their conversations by the pond. He was such a lovely child, so outgoing and friendly. She had seen him several times as a baby, snug in his pram. And then, that day, she had called by Katrina's and Marcus's house, only to see Marcus in the garden, Ben in his arms, just six months old. It had been such a stunning picture—Marcus in his T-shirt and shorts and Katrina in a long, floaty skirt, looking so much better with her arm lying lightly on Marcus's tanned forearm.

Jane took in a breath, changing gear sharply. Her world had changed that day. She had driven home without stopping, her love too great too hide, terrified they would see the resentment and dismay in her face.

Jane's red Peugeot reached the top of Westcliffe and a long road stretched ahead of her, flanked by impressive Victorian and Edwardian houses. Lights were on in many of them and at Hillcrest they glittered welcomingly through the sycamores bordering the long lawn.

Jane climbed from the car, smoothing down her new black dress and bolero jacket self-consciously, reflecting that the length seemed no more suitable now than it had when she had unpacked it. The hem was daringly well above her knees and the slim pencil skirt accentuated her long legs so that the strappy black shoes seemed almost too frivolous for the ensemble.

She knocked tentatively on the elegant front door, a stained-glass panel accentuating the warm lights from inside. While practising her first words to Marcus, Jane saw a figure run down the stairs and a small face peered out through the frosted glass.

'It's someone at the door, Dad!'

Jane spoke as Ben opened the door. 'Hello, Ben.'

'Dr Court!' Dressed in his pyjamas and wearing a pair of sunglasses, Ben bounced over the doorstep and into Jane's arms.

'My goodness.' She laughed. 'I didn't realise it was sunny this evening.'

Ben broke into a fit of giggles, tugging the over-large men's sunglasses, which were obviously his father's, from his nose. She had no option but to bend and give him a hug, and as she did so, Marcus followed down the stairs.

Jane's pulse raced as she recalled how Marcus always used to look in casual wear. His physique hadn't changed at all. Tall and rangy, he wore a dark green T-shirt with paint stains spattered across it and a pair of well-worn jeans that hugged his long, muscular legs.

'H-hello, Marcus,' she stammered, unable to hide the hitch in her voice as she gently prised Ben from her.

'Jane...this is a surprise. Is everything all right?' He pushed his dark hair from his face, hair that had small flecks of white paint embedded in it.

'I'm sorry to disturb you—I can see you're busy,' Jane apologised.

'Not at all. Come in.' He drew the boy gently back by the shoulder. 'Let Dr Court come in, Ben.'

'Dad's painting Mrs Barnes's bathroom for her,' Ben burst out, grabbing her hand and pulling her along. 'It used to have a lot of cracks in the ceiling but Dad's covered them all up, and I helped him. Come and see, come and see!'

'I'm sure Mrs Barnes is very pleased, Ben,' Jane said as she tried to come to a halt. 'But I don't want to disturb—'

'You're not disturbing us,' Marcus intervened, catching her eye. Laying his hands on Ben's energetic shoulders, he twisted his son towards him. 'Ben, settle down, now. I know you're excited, but Dr Court may not want to be dragged upstairs to the bathroom immediately—there may be another reason for her call, don't you think?' Marcus's amused grey eyes gazed enquiringly into the large round brown ones.

Ben nodded, his cheeks flushing under Marcus's gentle rebuke. He wore deep-blue pyjamas in a soft fleecy material and looked freshly scrubbed, a fact that was confirmed by Marcus, who drew his long fingers through the boy's thick, dark hair, capturing a small white fleck of paint.

'I think we missed a few bits here and there.' Marcus grinned as he glanced at Jane. 'But what we didn't extract in the bath tonight, no doubt will disappear in the next big shampooing session. Now, at the risk of a swift rejection, would you like to come upstairs and view the chaos?' His grey eyes went admiringly over her new dress. 'And on the way perhaps you can tell us why you've done us the honour of calling.'

But Jane had no time to respond as Ben pulled her up the stairs, his small bare feet padding rapidly on the carpet in front of her. When they breathlessly reached the bathroom, Marcus heaved with laughter.

'Now can you see the reason for the sunglasses?' Marcus chuckled.

Jane stared in at the bathroom, her eyes flinching as they were dazzled with a pure white brilliance. 'Well...it's...it's...very bright,' Jane gasped, trying to smother her laughter.

'Mrs Barnes was fed up with green,' Ben said very seriously, placing his spectacles on his small nose. 'She just wanted white all over. She's even going to have black and white tiles.'

'I'm sure it will look wonderful when it's finished,' Jane replied diplomatically, avoiding Marcus's amused gaze. 'Much better than green.'

'I'm reassured to hear it.' Marcus grinned. 'May we

come to you for treatment when the snow-blindness prevents us from differentiating black tiles from white?'

'Oh, absolutely. I've seen several cases of it already this year.' Jane giggled.

'Then we'll be in good hands,' Marcus replied, quirking an eyebrow.

At this they all burst into laughter, as Ben gave Jane a brief tour of the spotted white basin, loo seat and bath.

'Well, I think perhaps, young man,' said Marcus finally, 'we should offer Dr Court a cup of coffee in the comparative safety of the kitchen, don't you?'

Jane looked at Marcus and smiled. 'If you're not too busy…?'

His sudden smile was as heart-stoppingly breathtaking as ever, and Jane looked away quickly as he gestured to the stairs, Ben already bobbing ahead of them, chattering excitedly.

It was a quarter to eight before Jane finished her second coffee in the large, pine-filled kitchen which Mrs Barnes kept sparklingly clean. Marcus collected the paperwork from their quarters on the first floor as Ben tried to think up every excuse to persuade her to stay longer.

But Jane had put off leaving as long as she dared. She knew everyone was turning up at Cenna's house at eight, for eight-thirty drinks and buffet. Ben stood beside Marcus on the doorstep, the warm spring evening wafting wonderful scents into the air, making Jane pause as she turned to say goodbye.

She realised she didn't want to leave, her heart lurching as she thought of the long hours stretching ahead, talking with staff. An evening she would once have enjoyed, but now, after being in Marcus's and Ben's company, enjoying childish laughter and fun, the evening ahead held no attraction.

'Good luck with the snow-blindness,' she joked as she bent to receive a hug from Ben. 'I'm sure Mrs Barnes will be very pleased with the bathroom when it's finished.'

'You can come and see it, if you like,' Ben whispered in her ear, and her heart tugged again.

'Well…we'll see,' she murmured evasively. 'Don't forget your goggles.' She lifted the sunglasses from his pyjama pocket and perched them on his nose, tapping them gently into place.

'Tell Phil I'm sorry I didn't get them back to him in time,' Marcus said as she straightened up. 'Enjoy yourself this evening.'

'Thank you.' Jane met his gaze and felt awash with confusion. They had talked so easily tonight, about nothing in particular, but all the barriers had seemed to be down. In Ben's company they had been perfectly at ease, or was that, too, a mistake on her part? Yet now she was leaving and the barrier was up once more, his manner achingly polite, almost formal.

Hastily, she looked down at Ben and said quickly, 'Night, Ben, sleep well.'

She made a quick dash to the car, as fast as her slim black skirt would allow her, her strappy shoes clicking on the tarmac of the path. Lowering the folders to the back seat next to the box in which she had placed the desserts, she vaguely wondered if any of them had spoiled. But as she climbed into the driver's seat and switched on the lights, she forgot about her concerns as she bent her head and waved. Ben's small figure was still leaning against the taller one, as man and boy, silhouetted against the light, lifted their hands in reply.

The evening, Jane decided, had been a success. In all, twenty-two had attended, including the reception team, practice and district nurses and secretarial staff, along with their respective partners. Phil had displayed the plans, photos and general information in Cenna's conservatory and everyone had given their seal of approval. The evening had been filled with stimulated chatter and even a little music and dancing.

Cenna had also invited a few friends to her pretty new town house, built recently on a small estate just north of Nair. She had decided to use the occasion as a housewarming, five months after moving from her small flat in the town centre. As the last visitor left—Gaynor and her partner Tom, Jane helped Cenna clear away, her mind still drifting back to the house up on the cliffs.

'Stay and have a coffee,' Cenna tried to persuade her as Phil carried out the last of the rubbish to the garden.

But Jane shook her head as the day took its toll. 'Thanks all the same, Cenna, but I'm going to crash. It was a wonderful party. Everyone enjoyed it.'

'And all the food was eaten, save for a few sausage rolls.' Cenna smiled, pushing back her long dark hair from her flushed face. She had also bought a new dress for the occasion, a soft green silk shift that made her amber eyes look particularly lovely, Jane thought. Phil entered the kitchen door and came over, brushing down his grey chinos and light coloured shirt. Jane knew that this was the first time he had really socialised since his wife's death last year and, glancing at Cenna, she saw the look of concern in her eyes.

'Whew, that's the lot,' Phil said, sweeping back his thick, dark hair from his forehead. 'Is there anything more I can do, Cenna?'

'Stay for coffee if you've enough energy left.' Cenna smiled. 'Or a drink, if you prefer.'

But Phil shook his head. 'No, I'm driving, thanks, but a coffee will go down a treat. How about you, Jane?'

'No, but you two enjoy yourselves.'

Jane left them with a hug and drove the short distance home, relieved the evening had gone so well and rather glad now that she had bought her new dress. Everyone had dressed for the occasion, she thought wryly, and Cenna especially had looked lovely in her soft green dress. The thought crossed her mind that Cenna had also looked strangely different, too. Her expression had been a little distracted and Jane had seen her gazing across the room several times. Suddenly she thought of something and she wondered why it hadn't occurred to her before.

Cenna's gaze had gone to Phil—that was it! And just now, when she'd left, Cenna had had that same distracted expression, her cheeks flushed slightly under her dark hair. Jane smiled softly as she pulled up in her car and parked it in the road outside her cottage. Cenna—and Phil. Of course. Certainly, she had seen a look in Cenna's large amber eyes that day in the Fisherman's Haunt that she hadn't been able to translate—unlike Cenna, who had so astutely assessed the relationship between her and Marcus.

Jane leaned forward. Clasping her hands over the steering-wheel, she stared up into the midnight blue sky. The heavens abounded with stars and a crescent moon shone brilliantly above the rooftops. Out at sea, the reflection would have travelled over the water like a silver ribbon trembling in the breeze.

She sighed, thinking of Cenna and Phil and thinking also of Marcus and Ben. All the evening her thoughts hadn't really left them, up there in the cliff house. She could still feel Ben's small hand clasped around hers. Still see Katrina's huge dark eyes gazing back at her. Still feel Marcus's presence…hear his voice…inhale the scent of him. And, most vividly of all, remember what it was like to be taken in his arms and loved.

*   *   *

Towards the end of the following week Mr Macauley arrived at the surgery by courtesy of Yellow Car Cabs. He looked distressed as he entered Jane's room, his thin white hair in disarray and his perennial mac and baggy trousers decidedly the worse for wear. Knowing that he refused all help with the household chores and still catered for himself, Jane had always admired the way he turned himself out.

Peering through his thick spectacles, he fumbled for the chair. Jane was already on her feet, attempting to help him, although normally he refused such attempts. To her surprise he allowed her to guide him.

'How can I help, Mr Macauley?' she asked, having to speak louder and repeat her question as the elderly man gestured irritably to his ear. Having repeatedly refused to wear a hearing aid, the staff had accustomed themselves to shouting in his presence.

'I've got a pain here,' her patient grumbled, laying his hand on his stomach. 'It keeps me awake at night.'

'How long have you had it?' Jane asked.

'Oh, a long time. But don't you tell me I should have come sooner, because I know you people. You're only too eager to hand out pills of one sort or another.'

'Only when it's necessary, Mr Macauley. Now, can you describe this pain?'

'What's that?' The older man leaned forward.

Jane repeated her question.

'A pain is a pain. What do you mean, *describe* it?'

Jane tried to reason with her patient, but the interview became more fraught and she knew that her request to examine him would prove futile.

'I wish I hadn't come,' the old man muttered aggressively. 'I'm wasting my time talking to you people. I'll take some more stomach powders and be done with it.'

'What sort of stomach powders have you been taking?' Jane asked in surprise.

But the old man was already clambering to his feet. 'None of your business' was his abbreviated reply. Tottering towards the door, he fumbled for the handle.

Jane attempted to help him, but before she could he missed his footing, falling heavily towards the wall. She heard a crack and his cry of agony and knew before she arrived by his side that he had injured himself.

Almost at the same time, the door opened and Marcus stepped in. 'What the—?' he muttered as he rushed over to Jane as she knelt by the prostrate figure. Grasping the old man's outstretched arm, Marcus took it, relieving Jane of the weight.

'My...my hip,' gasped Mr Macauley. As he tried to move he let out another cry and Marcus glanced at Jane.

'I think we'll have to call an ambulance.'

Jane nodded and, leaving Marcus to attend to her patient, she dialled the emergency number.

'How did it happen?' Marcus asked as Jane knelt beside them again.

'I think he tripped,' Jane said on a sigh. 'I was too late to help him.'

'That's bad luck,' Marcus said quietly, supporting the old man in his arms. 'Just hang on there, Mr Macauley, we'll soon have you feeling more comfortable.'

Jane glanced at Marcus as his arm brushed hers. His touch seemed to burn through her sleeve and she jumped, her body tensing. Immediately the years rolled away, and with his touch it was as if the pain and heartache had never been. She didn't speak as she listened to Marcus reassuring Mr Macauley. She was back again at the hospital where they had trained and where their friendship had grown into love, when she had been naïve enough to plan a future to be shared with Marcus, a life that was to hold nothing but their happiness.

'Yes, I'm afraid the X-rays confirm a broken hip,' the casualty doctor told Marcus over the phone as Jane stood in his room the following day.

'When is he scheduled for an op?' Marcus asked.

'As soon as they can fit him in.' Marcus mouthed the reply to Jane while he listened to the comments of the doctor on the other end of the line. When he'd replaced the phone, he shrugged lightly. 'You know, while the old chap's in, they'll investigate the abdominal pain he was complaining of. A stay in hospital might prove opportune.'

'Yes, that's true,' Jane agreed thoughtfully. 'But I still feel dreadful he fell while with me.'

'If it had to happen somewhere, a doctor's surgery is possibly the right place,' Marcus remarked swiftly.

Jane nodded. 'Yes, I suppose so. Well, I'd better let you get on.'

Marcus spoke as she turned. 'You may see Ben trotting into surgery later. The bus is dropping him off here.'

'Oh, don't worry, I won't abscond with him again,' Jane was quick to assure him, but he frowned, shaking his head.

'Ben is rather eager to see you again.'

'Oh…really?' Her tone was uncertain as he gazed at her.

'You've been very kind to Ben.' Marcus smiled faintly. 'I worry that he really misses having a mother around. Has he ever spoken about it?'

She nodded as she met his gaze, pausing before she replied. 'A little. When we were sitting by the pool and having tea.'

Jane realised her willing participation in this conversation had inadvertently drawn her into the intimacy of the relationship they had shared with Katrina. There were so many things she hadn't understood then, and she understood them even less now. Had Marcus ever suspected that Katrina's attitude had changed after their marriage?

Marcus's gaze lingered on her. 'Has Ben mentioned—' he began, but as he was speaking the phone rang and she opened the door, nodding towards the desk.

'You're wanted,' she said quietly.

For a moment his eyes narrowed, but the insistent sound won, and with an almost audible sigh he reached out to the phone.

CHAPTER SIX

'So what does this mean, exactly?' Nancy Farlow asked Jane as she sat in her office the following week. 'What is basal cell carcinoma?'

Jane glanced at the results of the biopsy and then met her patient's gaze. 'Basal cell carcinoma is often referred to as rodent ulcers—you've probably heard of that name. It is a cancer of the skin, but can be treated extremely effectively, either by cauterisation, surgical removal or cryosurgery…even radiation.'

'Oh, God, that sounds heinous,' Nancy Farlow muttered, thrusting her hand through her blonde hair. Jane noticed she looked very drawn still, though she was once again wearing her make-up. 'Do you think this one under my eye is a rodent ulcer?'

'I have to say I do,' Jane replied.

'Am I likely to develop any more on my face?' Nancy asked after a pause.

'Certainly you should be aware of any new skin lesion or bump that arises.'

'What am I looking for—basically?' Nancy frowned. 'All moles look the same to me.'

'A skin lesion, growth or bump that looks pearly in appearance,' Jane explained. 'The colour varies from white or light pink to brown—or anything ulcerated, as you had before. Ultraviolet light is most intense at midday and people with your skin and eye colour are especially susceptible.'

'But why are they erupting now? If the sun has caused

76

it, why didn't they show up years ago?' Nancy asked anxiously.

'It doesn't work like that. Sometimes it takes years for the ulcer to appear after exposure to sun. There are other causes too—a genetic predisposition or exposure to arsenic which may be present in certain herbicides.'

'I've never had anything to do with arsenic or herbicides,' Nancy responded at once, 'and I don't know my real parents. I'm adopted. Both my adoptive parents have passed away—but they told me my mother was an unmarried girl who was unable to cope in her circumstances. I never traced her. I didn't feel the need. So I don't know what either my real mother or father looked like.'

'I see, well, although we won't be able to ascertain the reason, I can say that with swift attention to these areas there should be no reason why we can't clear them up,' Jane reassured her patient.

Nancy lifted her eyes. 'Well, what's a few more holes going to matter? And I'm still not working—so I suppose I should be grateful they haven't appeared while I'm in employment.'

'I think you will always need to examine yourself regularly for any changes,' Jane warned. 'You seem prone to this problem and it would be wise to keep one step ahead.'

Nancy sighed. 'Now, when do you want to see me next?'

'Tomorrow is Wednesday…Friday small ops clinic will be fine. I'm sure we'll have a spot for you.'

Nancy picked up her bag and smiled as she walked to the door. 'I'm sure you will. And I haven't got a reason now to argue with you. My time, it appears, is my own.'

When her patient had gone, Jane glanced at the notes she had made and she was still deep in thought as a knock came at the door and it opened slowly.

A small face peeped around and two dark eyes met hers. 'Ben?' Jane glanced at her watch. 'I didn't realise, it's three-thirty already.' She had to admit she looked forward to Ben's occasional visits, though more often than not they were only for the duration of a few minutes.

'Dad says I'm not to bother you,' Ben told her, entering under an abundance of schoolbags and a blazer that looked decidedly hot as he pushed his dark hair from his face. 'But the lady at the desk said I could come in for a moment as your next patient hasn't arrived.'

'It's always nice to see you, Ben,' Jane said warmly. 'Did the school bus drop you off?'

The boy nodded as he flopped down onto the chair. Lifting his large brown eyes, Jane could hear the slight wheezing in his chest.

'Have you your inhaler with you?' Jane asked and he nodded, bringing out the object from his blazer pocket. When he had used it, he sat back in the seat, chewing on his lip. 'I was wondering if I could come and see Donovan?' he asked breathlessly.

Jane paused. What was she to do? However much she tried to tell herself to keep a distance between Ben and herself, it was becoming increasingly difficult. But before she could decide on an answer, Ben was once again preoccupied with a search through his bag. After much struggling, he pulled out a crumpled paper bag. 'I bought him a present, 'cos his old one wasn't very good.'

Jane felt her throat constrict as she watched him push a blue felt strap across her desk. There was a shiny tin plate and small bell secured to the blue felt. Jane lifted the collar, reading the short inscription 'Donovan Court', followed by Jane's home phone number.

'Dad had it engraved.' The boy's eager gaze held Jane's. 'But I chose the bell and paid for it with my pocket money. Dad said it was only dogs usually that have name tags, but that you wouldn't mind.'

'Of course not, Ben. I...I'm sure Donovan will love it.'

'Can I put it on him?'

It was a request that Jane couldn't refuse and, returning the collar to Ben, she nodded. 'Yes…yes…of course. But you must ask—'

'Dad said you would say that I had to ask him first. So I asked him and he said if you said yes, then it was all right.'

So what was she to do now? she wondered. If Marcus had given his consent then all she could do was agree. But before she could respond Ben had jumped from his chair and come around the desk to stand beside her.

'I could come on Saturday if you like,' Ben said eagerly. 'Dad's on call, but he'll drop me off at your house, if it's all right.'

Jane knew she had no way of resisting the dark brown eyes that stared so earnestly at her. She nodded slowly. 'Yes, that's fine with me, Ben. But had you better make certain with Dad that Saturday is convenient?'

Ben grinned, brushing his fringe from his eyes. 'I already did,' he told her eagerly.

Later in the week Jane confirmed the arrangement with Marcus, rushed as they were with full surgeries. Marcus nodded his assent as they stood in the office, only pausing to say that he hoped Ben hadn't made a nuisance of himself.

On Jane's second Saturday morning on duty, her patients were few and fairly straightforward. By eleven-thirty she was ready to leave and stopped off in Nair town centre to shop for Ben's tea. She had no idea how long he would stay. The arrangement seemed to be open-ended, and when Marcus arrived with Ben he was in the process of dashing off to a call.

'Can he stay for tea?' Jane asked as Ben scampered through to the garden and Marcus stood on the doorstep.

He wore light summer trousers and a pale blue T-shirt, emphasising his deep tan. His black hair was freshly show-ered and lay damply across his head, a drift of his cologne wafting over on the breeze. Without warning, Jane felt the same old magic return, the coil of excitement tightening in her chest, the faint breathlessness that she had to control as she added uncertainly, 'Or would you like me to return him earlier?'

'No, if you're certain you can spare the time.'

'It's such a lovely day. I thought we might walk down to the harbour, take a picnic along to one of the coves.'

'I didn't think to bring any swimming trunks or sun-screen.' Marcus frowned.

'Oh, I wasn't thinking of swimming.' Jane shrugged. 'Just a slow walk and something to eat by the cliffs.'

'I'm envious,' Marcus said with a grin. 'It's the perfect day for a picnic.'

'You're welcome to join us,' Jane said before she could think about what she was saying. Wishing that she could retract it, she was surprised to see Marcus's smile widen.

'I'd love to, though I'll still be on call. Which beach were you thinking about going to?'

Jane shrugged. 'I'm not sure. Cutter's Cove probably, the nearest one to the Fisherman's Haunt. You can park in the pub car park and walk down to the sea. It's only about a hundred yards.'

'All right. I'll see how things go. But if I don't meet up with you, what time shall I call for Ben?'

'Oh, I'll drop him back later, if you like,' Jane offered. 'Say sevenish?'

Marcus nodded, then called out goodbye to his son, who shouted back from the garden. For a moment his eyes were drawn back to Jane's, the clear grey pools remaining steadily on her, their thick black lashes framing them with an intimacy that made Jane's heart leap.

As he walked to the car, Jane closed the door and leaned against it. Why had she invited him to join them? And what good could come of it? Already she'd broken the promise to herself of keeping at a distance.

Walking slowly through the hall to the lounge and then to the French windows, she looked out to see Ben curling the blue collar around Donovan's fluffy tabby neck. The cat sat quite still as Ben completed the manoeuvre, then, arching his back and purring noisily, the animal sprang up on the wall. Jane felt that odd little flutter inside her as Ben giggled delightedly and settled down by the pond to watch Donovan preen in the sun.

Cutter's Cove proved to be the perfect place for a picnic. Under the shelter of the tall, sandy-coloured cliffs, Jane spread out the contents of the hamper—fresh crusty bread, chicken drumsticks, wedges of cheese, a selection of fruit and large ripe red tomatoes stuffed with a tuna filling. Ben sampled everything, then explored the outcrop of rocks close by, his peaked cap pulled down over his forehead.

Jane had dressed in jeans, too, and resurrected her cap, pulling her hair back into a ponytail beneath. They searched for crabs and other treasures, discovering some pearly shells and cuttlefish. With a plastic bag crammed full, Ben jumped from one rock to another, his attention fully absorbed.

At four o'clock Jane spread out refreshments, calling to Ben. She had been on tenterhooks wondering if Marcus would appear and she was relieved that he hadn't. She had enjoyed the afternoon scouring the rocks with Ben—much more than she had anticipated.

'It's really nice, living by the sea,' Ben chattered as he sat cross-legged on the large tartan rug, hungrily devouring a ham sandwich. 'Where we used to live in London, there wasn't any sand or shells or anything. Daddy used to take me to the park and they had a sand pit and open-air swimming pool. But it wasn't like the seaside. I wish we could stay here.'

Jane poured fresh squash into a beaker, wondering what plans Marcus had for the future, but as curious as she was she didn't intend to engage Ben in a discussion on their future. However, Ben had other ideas.

'When I asked Dad why we couldn't,' Ben continued eagerly, 'he said 'cos we haven't got a *real* house here, not like we had in London with Mummy. He says next time we move we're going to stay at for a long, long time because of school and everything.'

'Well, I'm sure wherever it is, you'll like it,' she answered hesitantly, handing him the beaker.

'I won't like it as much as Nair,' Ben protested immediately. 'I won't like anywhere as much as I like it here.'

Jane felt her heart squeeze as she studied the wide brown eyes and thick dark hair framing the child's earnest face. He gave a little cough and, despite trying to distract his attention from the topic of leaving Nair, his breathlessness became worse.

'Here's your inhaler, Ben.' Jane opened her bag, disappointed that she had to resort to the inhaler when the day had been going so well. 'Now, just try to relax.'

'I wish we could stay here for ever,' Ben said wheezily. 'I wish...wish...'

Jane nodded, urging him to remain silent for a moment as he used his inhaler. A cool breeze suddenly swept off the sea and Jane decided it was time to leave. As soon as Ben had recovered his breath, Jane discovered an incentive to return in Donovan and by the time they reached the car she was relieved to note that Ben's asthma had completely cleared.

At home they found Donovan curled in his favourite spot by the pond. The big tabby stirred to welcome them, winding himself around their legs with a loud purr. While Ben washed and brushed up in the bathroom, Jane changed from her jeans and T-shirt into cream canvas trousers and a cool beige shirt.

Emptying the shells into a bowl, she left them to soak away the sand. Then she made hot chocolate in tall mugs and carried them into the garden. The courtyard was warmed by the afternoon sun and, slipping off her beach mules, she padded barefoot over the heated stones and reclaimed her thongs from the doorstep, wiggling her toes luxuriously.

Soon Ben appeared, his dark hair combed neatly, his face rosy as he curled up beside her on the swing seat. They drank the delicious chocolate and laughed at Donovan who turned on his back and wriggled his way under the rockery plants. Only his long tail swishing to and fro remained in evidence.

Whether it was the fresh air or the warm drink that sent Ben off to sleep, she didn't know. But his small head grew heavy on her lap and she looked down, trailing her fingers softly through his damp hair. His breathing became even and there was no sign of the wheeze that had disturbed him earlier in the day.

Was it talking about leaving Nair that had disturbed him—or was it just coincidence? she wondered. Gently sliding from the seat, she laid his small head on one of the cushions, managing not to disturb him. Pulling a throw over the small shoulders, she tucked it cosily around him.

After she had cleared away, the front doorbell rang and she answered it. Marcus stood there, looking slightly harassed. 'Sorry I didn't make it to Cutter's Cove,' he apologised as he stepped in. 'It was one of those afternoons.'

'I guessed you'd been kept pretty busy,' she answered as she led the way to the lounge. 'Would you like coffee or a cold drink?'

'No, thanks, I shan't stop.' Marcus ducked his head under the low beams. 'I merely thought I would save you the trouble of bringing Ben up to the house.'

'It wouldn't have been a problem,' she said with a shrug as she led him through to the lounge. 'But he fell asleep on the garden seat and I didn't like to disturb him. Unfortunately he had a brief asthma attack while we were on the beach.'

Marcus frowned at her. 'How bad was it?'

'Quite short in duration, fortunately. Once he'd used his inhaler he recovered.' She gestured to the garden and the sleeping form of Ben on the seat. 'Shall I wake him?'

Marcus shook his head slowly, his gaze softening at the sight of his son. 'No, leave him for a few minutes more. Perhaps I'll take you up on that coffee...if you don't mind.'

'Of course not. Make yourself comfortable here—or come into the kitchen if you like.'

He followed her through to the kitchen and as she put on the coffee percolator he said, 'I've just called on the Porchers—your patients, I believe.'

'Yes.' Jane nodded. 'At least, Sue Porcher is.'

Marcus nodded as he leaned one broad shoulder against the wall. 'She's booked to go in for her hysterectomy on Monday, but she seems to have some kind of virus.'

'What are her symptoms?' Jane asked.

'Sickness and temperature...though I have to say when I examined her it was only slightly up. However, if she's still sick tomorrow, I think she will have to let the hospital know. I said I would call again some time in the afternoon.'

'I'll go,' Jane said at once as he turned to look at her.

'Any reason why?' Marcus frowned.

'I can't be specific...but, you know, Sue really wanted to avoid a hysterectomy.'

'And you think she's deliberately stalling,' Marcus asked in surprise.

'No, I'm not saying that, but I do know her well—'

'And I don't?' Marcus interrupted coolly. 'At least not well enough to decide whether she's really unwell or having me on?'

'I didn't say that, Marcus—'

'Which actually reminds me that I wanted to talk to you about my on-call duties. I noticed that you are doing two consecutive call weekends.'

Jane nodded slowly. 'I'm quite happy about that—'

'You may be, but I'm not,' Marcus broke in again. 'My role as locum involves an equal share of the practice work. I don't need any favours—or to be reminded that my contract is temporary.'

'Marcus, that's unfair. I was thinking of Ben,' Jane protested as he frowned at her.

'*Ben*?' Marcus muttered darkly, his frown deepening. 'Ben is my responsibility.'

'I'm aware of that,' Jane responded crisply, hot colour flowing to her cheeks. 'I can see quite clearly that you're independent, Marcus, and that you don't need my help. But I refuse to be blamed for being absent from his life—which, if I'm not much mistaken, is what's really bothering you, isn't it?'

'Not for being absent,' he said in a low tone as his grey eyes went reproachfully over her face, 'but for leaving without telling me *why* you were going. For God's sake, Jane, imagine what it was like for me—one day you were there, as much a part of my life as Katrina and Ben, then the next gone. Vanished. What in heaven's name did you think I felt like?'

Jane stared at him, her voice shaking as she spoke. 'You and Katrina had each other, and Ben…a life together—'

'Which you were part of,' Marcus interrupted once more. 'I had a wife with leukaemia and a small son to care for.

Ben was, after all, the reason Katrina and I married—the reason you and I, Jane, gave up our future.'

'I know, but—' Jane broke off with a sound in her voice that was suspiciously like a gulped sob. As hot tears pricked her eyes, she turned away, placing her hand over her mouth. He was obviously unaware that Katrina had rejected their friendship, and even if she was to try to tell him now, would he believe her? How could she explain how Katrina had made it clear that she'd no longer been welcome at their home without sounding as though she was blaming Katrina?

'Jane…?' Marcus's voice came over her shoulder, the tenderness in it making her want to weep. Placing his hands on her shoulders, he turned her slowly around and she was powerless to stop him as he lifted her chin and gazed into her eyes. With the tip of his finger he drew away the escaped tear that was about to roll down her cheek. Drawing her towards him, she felt his lips cover hers in a kiss so familiar that the anger and recriminations were instantly forgotten.

'I'm sorry, Jane, don't cry…' he whispered against her hair. Without intending to her arms went around his shoulders, their breadth and strength so familiar that she felt as though she had never been out of his arms.

Closing her eyes, she felt the sweet taste of his mouth, the delicious opening of his lips over hers, and the passion instantly flared. All the potency their love-making had ever possessed was still there. Nothing had changed. Not the way he held her, or the way her body fitted against his, or the touch of his fingers on her skin, making her tremble with an aching desire that she recalled so well. Nothing had diminished in intensity. The feel, the smell, the taste of him were exactly as she had known them and had taken such pains to forget.

'Oh, Jane,' he muttered against her lips. 'Jane, what happened to us, what went wrong?'

She couldn't answer him, for the truth hurt too much. That it had been because he'd fallen in love with Katrina that everything had gone wrong. He would probably deny it—or would he? she wondered confusedly. As an exemplary doctor and surrogate father to Ben, he hadn't failed Katrina as a husband. And failing to love Katrina seemed impossible to Jane, for she had loved her, too, in her own way. A way that only true friends understood if one of those friends had asked for the kind of help that Katrina had.

And the consequences of that request had changed their lives. Katrina hadn't expected to live. Her request that Marcus and Jane should take care of Ben when she died hadn't allowed for her own survival...

These thoughts rushed through Jane's mind as Marcus softly caressed her face with his fingertips, his whispered words hot against her skin. Yet nothing could prevent her body wanting him as desperately as she always had. All her unanswered questions, her doubts and fears were drowned in the desire that made her yearn to be made love to.

'Marcus...' she breathed as she lifted her face, opening her eyes to meet his, their silvery depths glimmering as he brought her firmly against him.

'Oh, dear God, Jane, I've missed you.' His voice was low as he spoke. 'Jane, we have to talk.'

She nodded as a small voice calling from the garden made them move quickly apart and seconds later Ben opened the French window. 'Dad, it was brilliant at the beach. We found lots of shells and things. Dr Court says I can take them home and paint them.'

'That's a good idea,' Marcus replied, thrusting a hand

through his hair. 'We'll give some to Mrs Barnes for her garden.'

'I'll wrap them for you, Ben,' Jane said as Marcus briefly met her eyes above Ben's head.

CHAPTER SEVEN

THE following Monday morning, dressed in a soft summer green dress, Jane added a string of delicate white pearls to her neck and small pearl studs to her ears. One thing she *was* certain of. She wanted to look as though she hadn't spent all weekend in an irrational state.

The chemistry was still there, the physical desire. She had honestly—and painfully—admitted that fact to herself. But she was a very different person to the young woman Marcus had once known. And the same had to be said for Marcus. He, too, had changed.

When Jane arrived at surgery, her concern was that she had made a fool of herself, and had Ben not been present on Saturday the situation might have got out of hand. What was the point of stirring up old memories, let alone raking over the past? she had asked herself afterwards.

She hadn't had time to think when Marcus had demanded to know why she'd left London, and her reply hadn't explained why she'd no longer been able to remain part of his and Katrina's lives.

With difficulty, Jane managed to put these thoughts out of her mind as she began her Monday morning surgery. Clyde Oakman was her first patient, though usually Phil was his preferred GP. A local fisherman and married with two boys, he had asked to be fitted in urgently.

'Caught my hand in the tiller,' he told her as he unwrapped his fingers from a blood-soaked bandage. 'Damn nuisance. Do you reckon I'll need stitches, Dr Court?'

Jane saw at once that the six-inch tear of skin was in need of repair. In the treatment room, she cleaned and froze the injury to palm and thumb and finally sutured the awkward tear. 'When did you do this?' she asked as she applied the final suture of a neat row.

'This morning, about fivish,' Clyde replied irritably. 'Just getting the pots ready to use I was…thought I'd check for seaweed clogging up the works. Damn nuisance—felt like razors, those shells. I thought I might get away with it at first, but when it kept bleeding I decided to nip in to see you lot.'

'Have you had a tetanus shot lately?' Jane asked.

'Nope, don't think I've had the pleasure.' Clyde laughed, a wide grin spreading across his red face. Under a thatch of sandy hair and cluster of holed jumpers he looked—and smelt—the proverbial fisherman. 'The last one I had must be over ten years ago,' he added after a moment's thought.

Jane checked the records and confirmed the need for a booster. She prepared the tetanus and swiftly administered it. 'Try to keep your hand out of water,' Jane warned. 'Though I know it will be difficult, given your trade.'

The big fisherman shrugged. 'I'll leave the heavy stuff to Brian. It'll give him something to do while he's moping around the place.'

'Brian Porcher?' Jane knew that the two often worked together.

'Yeah, he's a miserable devil lately. His missus don't think she's gonna be able to produce that son and heir he wants so much.'

Jane looked up and frowned. 'I didn't realise he wanted a son so badly.'

Clyde nodded. 'Who else is gonna run his boats for him? A bally team of women?'

Jane resisted the urge to say that the womenfolk were as much responsible for the success of their husbands' sea-going businesses as the men, since she knew that would spark the usual debate. However, she was dismayed to hear that Brian Porcher seemed to be little concerned for the welfare of his wife, who had given him six lovely daughters already.

'Cheerio, then, Doc, and thanks,' Clyde called as he left, whistling his way down the hall. Jane was staring thoughtfully after him when Marcus passed the open door.

'Hello, there,' he said quietly. Pausing, he looked into the room.

'Hi.' She hesitated as she removed her disposable apron and threw it into the bin. 'Is there something you want?'

'You're busy?' he asked, his tall frame filling the doorway.

'Not now.' She looked up. 'And you?'

'I've not too long a list, mostly TRs this morning...' He paused as though he was about to say something else. 'Er, look, Jane—'

'And Ben?' she interrupted quickly, moving back to the bench, aware that he was watching her. 'How is he this morning?'

'A little wheezy, but he was OK. However...' Marcus paused, frowning. 'I'm afraid we've had one or two upsets lately that seem out of character,' he added hesitantly.

Jane gave a small shrug. 'Well, he might be anxious about school or—' She stopped, recalling the attack of asthma which had followed Ben's remark about wanting to stay in Nair.

'Yes...go on,' Marcus prompted. 'Has he said something to you?'

Jane turned away slightly from his gaze. 'I don't know whether it bore any relevance to what you're talking about...'

'Even so, I'd like to know.' Marcus walked slowly towards her and she had no option but to meet his curious gaze. She wondered why it was that she was so unlike her normal self in his presence. He seemed to have the knack of making her feel vulnerable, and she sharpened her tone more than she intended.

'Ben was talking to me about Nair and the seaside…and how he wasn't looking forward to leaving. It was then that his asthma attack began.'

'Jane, the boy has been suffering from asthma for two years,' Marcus protested at once. 'It can't have a bearing on our current situation.'

'Not directly,' she agreed, 'but he certainly loves the sea. And wasn't that one of the reasons why you decided to come to Nair? To discover whether or not the environment helped?'

'Yes, that's true.' Marcus's grey eyes were cool. 'But so far there's not been a great deal of improvement, as you yourself witnessed.'

'Even a small improvement is better than nothing,' she replied quietly. Realising the atmosphere was becoming tense between them, she bit her lip and turned towards the door.

But just as she moved Marcus reached out for her arm. 'Jane, I'm sorry. I didn't mean to bite your head off.'

She was aware of his grip and as her eyes met his she saw he meant his apology. His gaze softened under the worried frown pleating his forehead. 'Marcus, I'm not trying to pry. I know it must be very difficult for you, dealing with Ben's asthma, and whatever you do, you do it for Ben's sake—'

'And I'm defensive about him, I know.' Marcus made a sudden attempt at a smile. 'It hasn't been easy bringing Ben up. I haven't been able to fill the vacuum Katrina left. And I want Ben to feel secure, though possibly the way I'm going about it doesn't seem sensible to an outsider.'

Jane stared at him in dismay. 'Is that how you think of me, as an outsider?'

He shook his head quickly, his other hand coming up to

grip her arm and draw her close. 'Of course not. I didn't mean that. Jane, do you think we could possibly find time to talk? I don't mean here. I mean by ourselves. Somewhere on neutral territory, where we can sit and have a quiet chat. I think, after what happened on Saturday, we owe it to ourselves, don't you?'

Suddenly the friction that had been between them seemed to melt away as she gazed into his eyes and saw the sadness there. For a moment she was silent, her heart pounding as he held her. 'I…I just don't know what good talking over the past will do, Marcus,' she stammered. 'What happened on Saturday was a mistake.'

'Was it?' He refused to let her go and his grip tightened. 'I know you felt something, Jane.'

'Marcus, all I know is for a moment or two, we…we lost control.'

'All right. I agree with you. But if we did, why was the control there in the first place? Surely if we no longer felt an attraction towards one another, I wouldn't have kissed you and you wouldn't have kissed me back.'

'Marcus, I—' she began as she tried to pull away, but he held her and she had no way of disguising the colour that flooded into her face.

'Just a quiet drink,' he said in a low, urgent voice. 'We can't go on like this, Jane. You must see that.'

It was the sound of footsteps approaching that forced her to nod and close her eyes briefly in agreement. When she flicked them open again, he let his hands slip away, his fingertips still having the power to make her tremble as they skimmed her bare flesh.

His eyes met hers as the door drifted open and Annie looked around it. 'Oh, Dr Granger, there you are.' The receptionist gave a momentary smile and, glancing hesitantly from one to the other, added, 'Could you take one more temporary resident tacked onto the end of your surgery?

There's a five-minute slot, but I know you wanted to get away on your calls...'

'No problem, Annie,' Marcus answered quietly. 'As long as I'm away before lunch.'

'Oh yes, we'll make sure you are,' Annie promised, and with a relieved smile hurried back to Reception.

For a moment they remained staring at each other, Jane wondering what she had done in agreeing to meet him, but how could she have refused? If not for the sake of their working relationship, then at least for Ben's she had to try to come to some kind of understanding over the next few months. If that meant a civilised drink somewhere in relative peace and quiet, what harm could it do?

'Where?' Marcus asked her, his hand on the door. 'And when?'

'I...I don't know,' she murmured, her voice shaky. 'What about Ben?'

'I'll ask Mrs Barnes when she'll next be free,' Marcus answered quickly. 'But shall we say tentatively some time this weekend—Cenna's on call, I believe.'

Jane nodded and with a hesitant smile, his eyes meeting hers, Marcus left the room, his tall figure disappearing out of the door and along the passage to his room.

On Thursday afternoon, Jane drove to Southampton. As it was her day off and she had been concerned for Mr Macauley, her intention was to visit her elderly patient and enquire about his rehabilitation post-op. She had phoned Social Services to discover whether they were in full possession of his details, and because he had fallen while in the process of a consultation Jane couldn't help but feel responsible.

It was a beautiful June day and the weather held all summer's promise. An hour's slow drive along the coast road gave her the opportunity to clear her mind, but her thoughts inevitably returned to Marcus. They had agreed to meet on Saturday, arranging the time for seven at the Fisherman's Haunt.

As she drove, yet again she questioned her judgement. How easy it would be to respond to Marcus, given the right circumstances. She had allowed him to kiss her and knew that in those moments she had lost all touch with reality. They had been back again as students and his touch and feel had been the same as it had ever been. There was no doubt they had wanted each other then…but what could it achieve, to resurrect any relationship between them?

Marcus had chosen to marry Katrina—and she, Jane, had supported that decision. But they were different people now, a long way from the carefree youngsters who had fallen in love whilst training.

Jane parked in the hospital car park and made her way to the trauma ward where Mr Macauley was recovering. It was a small ward of six beds and Mr Macauley lay, fully dressed on the top of his, bolstered by pillows.

'Mr Macauley?' Jane bent over him, anxious not to wake him if he was asleep. But the closed eyes gradually opened and a flicker of recognition caused her to smile. 'It's Dr Court,' she said softly, lowering a bag of grapes to the locker. 'How are you feeling?'

With an effort the elderly man eased himself up on the pillows. His shirt looked clean and tidy and he was freshly shaved. 'What have you come for?' he demanded in a gruff tone.

'To visit you,' Jane responded, prepared for the un-friendly response. 'I understand your surgeon has fitted you with a new hip?'

'Feel like a chicken trussed up at Christmas,' the elderly man muttered. 'At my time of life, you'd think they'd just let me fade away.'

'No one is going to do that,' Jane replied with a wry smile.

'Of course we're not,' the staff nurse said as she brought a Zimmer to the side of the bed. 'We have a bed for you in another unit later today, Mr Macauley. Physio will be able to help you more—ten minutes a day of exercise and you'll be as good as new. That is, once the doctor's attended to your hernia.'

'Hernia?' Jane looked at her patient in surprise, then glanced back at the nurse. 'So a hernia was the problem?'

'Big as a golf ball,' Mr Macauley announced loudly. 'You lot at the surgery should have known—don't know how you managed to miss it.'

'Possibly because you never gave us the opportunity to examine you,' Jane replied ruefully, and the staff nurse grinned.

'There, that's what I said, didn't I, Mr Macauley? Now, if you look at that young man over there, he'll tell you another story…about how if it wasn't for these good doctors of Nair surgery he wouldn't be here today.'

Jane glanced across the ward at a young man in the bed opposite. With a start, Jane recognised him, despite the recently shaven head and gaunt features. The last time she'd seen him had been when he'd been lying trapped in his car and Marcus had been attempting to staunch the blood coming from a wound in his leg.

'Timothy Lister,' Staff said to Jane. 'The young man who had an accident near your surgery. And he can't sing your praises loud enough, which…' she turned and wagged a finger at the eighty-two-year-old '…just goes to show you what wonderful doctors you've got.'

'Can't hear a word you're saying,' barked Mr Macauley. 'You'll have to shout if you want me to hear.'

'Wasn't there another car involved? I seem to recall we had other casualties in at the same time.'

'Yes, three others.' Jane nodded. 'But I believe they have all recovered.'

'Well, why don't you go and say hello?' Staff suggested. 'You'll make his day.'

Jane nodded and as the nurse left she glanced back at Mr Macauley. 'I was wondering if Social Services have arranged any help for you when you come home?'

'Got 'em calling round every day apparently,' he responded shortly. 'Blessed nuisance. Don't like 'em poking their noses in, but I suppose I'll have to suffer it. One thing I'm not agreeing to is going into one of these old people's homes. They've been on about it, but it won't make no difference. I was born in the house I live in and that's where I'm going to die.'

Jane couldn't resist a smile. 'Well, I'll leave you to your physiotherapy session. There are some grapes on your locker. I thought perhaps you might like some fresh fruit.'

To Jane's amusement, a shaky hand reached out and clutched the bag, placing it on the bed in front of him. 'They don't look bad, I suppose,' he muttered. Then with a frown the elderly man looked up. 'You coming again?'

'Would you like me to?'

'Suit yourself,' Mr Macauley huffed. 'But if you do, I'd like tangerines next time.'

Jane smiled to herself as she left the bedside and walked over to Timothy Lister. Before she could speak he held out his hand. 'The nurse told me who you were,' he said at once.

'How are you?' Jane sat in the chair beside his bed.

'Better now,' he answered with a grin. 'I've been in Intensive and then in a side ward for so long I was beginning to forget what it's like to be with people.'

'Are you up and about?' Jane asked hesitantly.

'Not as much as I'd like, but I've got back the use of my legs. And the internal damage has healed. All this is

OK, too.' He shrugged, gesturing to the wounds on his head. Jane sensed he was still finding it difficult to adjust to what happened to him.

'It's weird I should end up in a ward with him.' Timothy nodded at the older man. 'Though I'm not blaming the old bloke. I know I was well out of order. If I'd kept under the speed limit, I'd've had chance to swerve.' He paused before adding slowly, 'I've got a bit of a problem with the police over that. I used to have bikes, pretty fast ones. Then I went on to cars. Been pulled up for speeding before and, well, I think I'll lose my licence this time.'

'I see. Well, I'm sure after this you'll have second thoughts before speeding in any vehicle.'

'I've learnt my lesson.' He sighed wearily. 'But a bit too late.'

'It's never too late,' Jane said as she looked back at the younger man. 'You're lucky to be alive, as I'm sure you know.'

Timothy nodded. 'I don't remember much, but the police told me what happened. Will you thank the doctor who helped me? What was his name?'

'Dr Granger. And, yes, I'll pass on your message.' She glanced at Mr Macauley. 'I may be visiting again, so perhaps I'll see you then.'

'Is he a relative of yours…the old man?'

'No. But he fell and broke a hip in my consulting room.'

Timothy frowned. 'He should have a health warning attached to him.'

'I'm sad to say he has no one interested enough to care about his health,' Jane replied as she glanced back at Mr Macauley. 'That's why I came in today.'

'Perhaps he'll cheer up a bit now he's had a visitor,' the young man murmured.

Jane smiled. 'Yes, perhaps. He's extremely short-sighted

and rather deaf, so that makes it even more difficult for him to socialise.'

When she left the hospital, Jane reflected that Timothy seemed genuine in his desire to change his ways. Though Mr Macauley had been partly to blame in crossing the road at a snail's pace, a vehicle travelling at a slower speed would have managed to brake. Obviously, the young man's track record was now going against him and she hoped that he really meant what he said regarding his future attitude to driving.

She took the road toward Southampton city centre and parked in a multi-storey car park. She had a vague idea of doing some shopping; Saturday presented a problem she had avoided setting her mind to. What could she wear? The new dress she had worn to the office party was the obvious choice, but Marcus had seen it. Not that it was important to her whether he had or not. But if that was true, she asked herself as she locked her car and set off for the shopping centre, why bother to give the matter a second thought?

She decided, recklessly, on another new dress. Trying to convince herself that two new dresses in one month was the result of two years of neglect of her wardrobe, Jane still couldn't ease her conscience. By Saturday morning she was still trying to convince herself of the sense of meeting Marcus. By Saturday evening, she was still uncertain as to whether to wear the new dress.

When she tried it on, however, the simple cut and cornflower blue of the soft material felt so appropriate to the gorgeous summer's evening she knew she had made the right decision. The dress slipped over her slim hips and long legs as though it had been made for her, rather than randomly off the rack. The sleeveless bodice with its plain round neckline looked cool and unfussy and gave her the opportunity to twist up her hair into a knot.

Leaving several soft wisps of silky blonde hair to fall

around her face, she sprayed on the last of her favourite perfume. Teaming the dress with fashionable darker blue mules, she felt confident enough to walk into the Fisherman's Haunt and for a moment pause, her gaze moving slowly over the crowd huddled around the bar.

Several men turned to glance her way and for a moment she wondered if Marcus would turn up. His suggestion of collecting her had been swiftly refused—it would only have meant he'd have to drop her back and that would pose the question of asking him in for coffee.

Suddenly someone touched her elbow. Jane turned to find Marcus looking down at her, and she felt a wave of relief. 'I was wondering whether you would turn up,' he said quietly.

Managing not to disclose her own doubts, she smiled. 'What made you think I wouldn't?' she asked as he took her arm.

'Just that I haven't seen you much since we made the arrangement. I thought you might have been trying to avoid me.'

'You know me better than to break an arrangement,' she said, praying he wasn't aware of the nervousness in her voice.

He nodded, his grey eyes meeting hers. 'That's what gave me hope.' He grinned. 'I've found us a seat over there, by the window. Will that do?'

'Yes, perfectly.'

From the corner of her eye Jane took in his appearance as they walked. He looked taller and darker than ever, as though he'd just come back from some exotic holiday. But that, she realised, was because his skin tanned so swiftly and his thick dark hair looked more luxurious than ever against an ivory polo shirt and light chinos.

They settled at a table overlooking the harbour, on the other side of the room to where she'd sat with Cenna. But

the view was just as breathtaking, and in the late evening
sunshine there were several fishing boats pulling up to the
side of the quay. Marcus ordered them soft drinks as both
of them were driving and asked whether she would like to
eat. She refused, not because she had eaten but because the
knot in her stomach was tight enough to counteract any
enjoyment she might have had of a meal.

'I've eaten, too,' he said as he lowered his drink to the
table and crossed his long legs. 'But it was just a thought.'

'Did Ben know you were meeting me tonight?' she
asked, sipping her Perrier, grateful for the sharp tang of
lemon on her tongue.

'Yes, I told him.' His eyes went over her, taking in the
soft arch of her neck and the silky fronds of hair that curled
softly around her ears. 'You look beautiful tonight,' he
added softly. 'The colour of that dress…it's the same as
your eyes.' He lifted his gaze and stared at her. 'Jane…I
don't know where to start to repair the damage. I only know
I want to try. If it's not too late…if we can…' He shrugged
his broad shoulders under the polo shirt, his muscular frame
moving the material with a sensual ripple that Jane recalled
so clearly.

She looked down at her glass and knew that even if she
tried to swallow the liquid in it at this moment, she
wouldn't be able to. Her throat felt tight and her mouth dry.
The effect he had on her hadn't changed in the least.
Marcus was still the man he always used to be. The chemistry was still there and there was no way she could deny
it.

But where was the sense in all this? a small voice wailed
inside. She had been down this road before, loved him so
passionately that life had meant nothing without him. How
could she expose herself to the dangers again, knowing the
penalty to be paid?

'Jane?' He leant forward, his voice dropping beneath the

murmur of voices in the room. He reached toward her hand and softly took hold of it. She trembled under its grip and gently drew away, terrified he would see the vulnerability in her eyes.

He shrugged slowly and rested back in his chair, dropping his head slightly. 'After you left London, I tried to find you, to tell you what was going on in our lives.'

'As I said, what good would that have done, Marcus?' she murmured, her voice catching. 'You were married to Katrina. You had adopted Ben as your own. And Ben was the reason we did it, wasn't he?'

Marcus looked up sharply. 'Of course he was. Why else would I have agreed to marry Katrina? You don't think... You—' He stopped short, the pleat in his forehead deepening as he sat forward. 'Jane, is that why you left—because you thought that Katrina and I had feelings for one another?'

Jane averted her gaze from the question in his eyes.

'Katrina was pregnant and ill and she asked us for help. We gave it, because no one else was there for her. James was dead and she was alone. I had no intimate feeling for Katrina—surely you couldn't have thought there was more to our relationship? We were friends, Jane...*friends*.'

'I...I know that,' Jane murmured, still unable to meet his gaze.

He took hold of her wrist and gripped it hard. 'Look at me, Jane.'

She turned her face up towards him and for a long, agonising moment he gazed deeply into her eyes.

'It might have been different if her parents had volunteered their help,' he muttered, searching her face as he spoke. 'But they didn't want the child. What could we do, Jane?' Marcus's gaze was unflinching. 'Katrina risked her life to give birth to Ben. She could have had treatment but she refused, and both you and I knew—as her closest friends—there was no hope.'

With a shudder Jane recalled the letter Katrina had showed them from her parents. In a way she had understood their dilemma. They were elderly, having had Katrina, their fourth child, in their forties. The father had been sick at the time Katrina had been pregnant, and Katrina's news hadn't helped the already distant family relationship.

'Ben meant so much to her,' Marcus murmured, his grip tightening. 'He was all she had left of James.'

'And us?' Jane whispered bleakly. 'We were going to be married. We had our lives ahead of us. Our careers. We had made so many plans, were only beginning our lives together when James died.'

'I know,' he agreed quietly. 'Interrupting our life was a sacrifice, but we both decided to make it.'

Jane nodded slowly. 'I know you had special reasons, that Sara was adopted.'

His voice softened as he spoke of his sister. 'I remember how much it has always meant to her. My parents loved her as their own. You must know the only choice for me was to accept responsibility for Ben.'

'But as much as I loved Katrina...' Jane began hoarsely, attempting to try to explain the change in Katrina's attitude, but failing miserably. Instead she said, 'She...she became your wife.'

Marcus looked at her with confused grey eyes. 'Yes, she was my wife—but she was dying. I cared for her deeply, as you did, and knew that it would only be a matter of time before Ben was orphaned.' There was a long silence before he spoke again. 'None of us knew how long she would survive. It was only her determination to stay with Ben and try to create some memories for him that gave her the strength to carry on for that short while.'

Jane glanced up, aware of the softening of his tone as

he spoke of Katrina. Yet again it seemed as though it would be a betrayal of her friendship to explain the truth, the real reason why she had really left London. Katrina had been so brave and she had fully deserved to lead the rest of her short life in peace.

'I'm sure that's true,' she agreed quietly, and with his hand still clasped around her wrist they sat for a long time, both preoccupied with their own thoughts of the past. Then finally she cleared her throat and murmured, 'You introduced me to Ben as an old friend. How much does he know of our past?'

'Not a great deal.' His mouthed curved into a gentle smile. 'I've explained that his mother and you and I were all good friends. He really hasn't asked me very much more.'

'Does he know about James?'

'Katrina told him about the accident and his real father's death. But I believe he was too young to grasp the full meaning.' He paused, his strong fingers slipping around her hands as they lay on the table. 'He's always called me Dad. I still don't believe he's old enough yet to understand the full truth.' His voice was husky as he added, 'The time will come, I realise, when he will want to know more.'

'And will you tell him?'

Marcus gazed into her eyes. 'I'll tell him his mother was a wonderful woman and that she cared more for him than she did for her own life. And I'll tell him as much as I'm able to about James. As for you and I, I was hoping we could talk to him about the days when we were young and all friends. The happier times. He needs to know about those. To understand that his mother was a part of our history and was loved very dearly.'

It was no good trying to fob herself off with half-truths, Jane realised as she swallowed on the lump in her throat.

Marcus was asking for her help rather than suggesting she distance herself, as she had at first thought.

Could she refuse him, allow herself to become vulnerable again to the past she had fled from? How easy it would be to give in. How ready she was to say yes. And what madness it was to expose herself to such a risk...

But it was a risk her foolish heart seemed willing to accept as Marcus's fingers slipped into hers, and this time she didn't draw them away.

CHAPTER EIGHT

'It's a beautiful night.' Marcus held open the door for her as they left the Fisherman's Haunt. The sound of the waves lapping against the harbour walls broke the stillness as they stepped out into the twilight. A few holidaymakers strolled along the quay, but all the fishing vessels had tied up long ago and rocked gently on the tide.

'Yes...so many stars,' Jane breathed, looking up into the heavens. 'But, then, from Nair, on a clear night like this, it sometimes seems as though you can see the whole of the universe.'

'Do you remember when we said the same thing about London?' Marcus murmured as they strolled towards the car park. 'From the roof garden of your flat?'

Jane nodded, unable to look at him. The little flat that she and Katrina had shared as students had been unbearably cramped at times, but the roof garden had provided a wonderful escape. The four of them had spent many evenings there, talking till late into the small hours.

'I never thought I would find anywhere else to compare with it,' he added stiffly. 'But that was when we were younger and before James died. After that, everything changed.'

Jane swallowed hard. 'Our lives did change after James's death... I don't know what to say to you now. I never thought I would see you—or Ben—again.'

'Which is where I differed,' Marcus murmured as they came to a stop by her car. They were standing in the twilight, a full moon overhead slipping briefly behind a cloud. The shadowed face of Marcus looked like that of some

106

Greek god, his dark eyes and chiselled features taking her breath as she gazed up at him. 'I always thought there would come a time when our paths would cross. Like this…now…when we could talk about the past without rancour. I never meant to hurt you, Jane. You were the most important person in my life—but we had to make some difficult decisions.'

'Do you think they were the right ones?'

'Whether they were wrong or right, we made them.' Marcus reached out and lifted the long tendrils of blonde hair that wrapped around her face in the soft breeze. 'It's no use thinking there might have been another way—the present is what is important. This day, this moment…you and I standing here in the moonlight. It's almost as though time has never separated us.' His fingers lifted her chin and slowly he bent his head. 'Jane, you look so lovely, so beautiful…just as I remember…'

Before she could reply his lips came down on hers, softly at first as he drew her towards him. As her hands went up to his shoulders his arms went around her and the kiss deepened until she felt herself floating away. Nothing mattered then, not the past or the future, but, as Marcus had said, only the present and their need.

She moved against him and he groaned softly, slipping one hand down to her waist and holding her tightly, so that any thought of escape vanished from her mind. It was a kiss that returned her to the moment she had first known about herself, about the strength of her desire for one man. It was also a kiss that told her that nothing had lessened her passion for him.

On her indrawn breath her lips stung with the pressure lifted from them and she trembled, knowing she missed them the moment they were gone.

'Jane…' he whispered huskily, his breath fanning over

her cheek. 'Oh, Jane, have we changed that much from the people we used to be?'

'I—I think so.'

'But how? How, Jane?'

'I suppose now…I…I'm a little set in my ways…' she answered with brutal honesty as she stared up at him. 'I've only myself to think about.'

'And you've never wanted a family—children of your own?'

How could she explain that she had been forced to smother those longings without laying the blame for what had happened at his feet? Of course she had wanted babies—*his* babies. Having expected to marry Marcus herself, she had dreamed of a family of their own.

'Oh, Marcus…you don't understand.'

'Then make me understand,' he growled as his lips sought hers and the kiss they shared next was intense and deep, his tongue seeking the sweetness of her mouth, his hands pulling her roughly against him.

It was no ordinary kiss and she knew somewhere in her mind that responding to it left no need for the words she found so hard to say.

In the darkness of the hall, Jane waited breathlessly for Marcus to lock his car. She heard his soft footsteps up to the front door and with trembling fingers opened it wider. If she'd convinced herself that driving to the Fisherman's Haunt would stop events from escalating, then she had been a deluded fool.

She wanted him so much her body ached for him, and as he stepped over the threshold and scooped her into his arms she knew that nothing would have kept them apart tonight. Their passion overrode common sense and logic, just as it had when they had been younger.

When they'd first met, they'd known that there had been

something special between them. It had been indefinable, but it had been enough to distract her from her studies and for a while send them both onto a crazy path. Once James and Katrina had spent more time on their own, it had been evident that she and Marcus had been meant to do the same.

The initial hesitation in their romance had only made their eventual union more fulfilling. And as the months had gone by, every spare minute not spent studying had been spent in one another's company. Perhaps that's why they had felt so close to Katrina and James…

But it wasn't of Katrina and James that Jane was thinking as the front door snapped shut and Marcus pulled her into his arms. His kisses were hard and demanding on her lips as though to blot out any memory of their past.

Their stumbling steps to the bedroom were only halted as Jane rattled the latch on her bedroom door, fumbling her way in. Marcus pulled off his polo shirt, then swept her into his arms. His kisses hardly left her time to breathe, his hands claiming the soft roundness of her breasts, a groan coming from his throat as they sank to the bed.

'You looked so beautiful when you came in the pub to-night,' Marcus whispered as he lifted her effortlessly against him. 'I saw you and you took my breath away. I wanted you, Jane, I wanted you so much.'

He slid down the zip on the back of her dress, peeling the soft blue material from her shoulders. He stretched out beside her, his eyes, even in the darkness, going over her with desperate desire. The touch of his mouth on her bare skin made her shiver. She was barely holding on to the threads of her control as he began to undress her.

'Marcus, please…' But she didn't finish her sentence. His mouth was back again, forcing the breath from her lungs as his fingers unclipped her bra and sought her breasts with a frantic urgency.

She undid the belt of his chinos and soon they were

dropped to the floor, along with her clothes. Naked, they embraced, the world forgotten. Their loving was as wild as it had once been. Wilder perhaps, Jane guessed as in some part of her brain she registered the real world, blocking it out swiftly, sensually, as his body quivered, drawn as tight as a bow over her.

Her cries were muffled as his kisses rained over her body. She closed her eyes, abandoning all hope of self-control. She felt the soft scrape of the thick dark curls on his chest, running her fingers through them with an un-tamed delight. She gasped at the hard, taut muscle, the same animal energy that matched her own uniquely. She felt his soul reaching out to her and she answered it in the only way she knew how.

Their climax was swift and thundering, her cries shat-tered only by his as some force of nature decreed perfect timing. And it was only when he sank beside her that she allowed herself to look at him, to gaze lovingly into the darkened eyes before they fell asleep.

'Do…do you have to go?' she breathed as they woke in one another's arms and he curled her against him.

'Not yet.' He kissed her slowly. 'Do you want me to?'

'Of course not. I…I was thinking of Ben…'

He kissed her cheeks and her forehead softly, cupping her head into the crook of his neck. 'He's safe with Mrs Barnes. I don't want to leave you, Jane.' Two tender thumbs came slowly down to massage her nipples, arousing her once more as they grazed seductively over the tiny peaks.

'And I don't want you to go.' Her body responded at once and she reached up, taking his head between her hands. 'Kiss me, Marcus.'

He crushed her against him, their bodies still damp in the tangle of sheets. It was seconds only before their pas-

sion took over with fresh urgency as they began to make
love, teasing, arousing and, this time, enjoying all the old
memories of their love-making, while seeking the new.

Time had only added to their enjoyment, Jane realised
as she silently recalled and savoured his familiarity. The
hardness of his thighs and strength of his arms. The sexy
curve at the base of his backbone, the sudden jut of muscle
on his broad shoulders, the unexpected tenderness of his
agile fingers. The pain of separation slowly faded. The aching, lonely years were for a while obliterated. It was only
the here and now that counted.

As they made love again, Jane forgot the ghosts of the
past, putting out of her mind the possibility they might well
return tomorrow. It was, as Marcus had said, the present
that counted.

It was after one when Marcus left. He pulled on his clothes
and she dressed in her robe, walking down into the hall to
kiss him again as they stood in the dark. Reaching for the
door, she opened it reluctantly, but he held it and dragged
her into his arms.

'I still don't want to go,' he said roughly, holding her
face between his large hands. 'Jane, I—'

She knew that neither of them would have broken apart
had not some sixth sense told them someone was approaching. A couple came into view on the other side of the road,
fortunately too involved in themselves to notice anyone
else.

Marcus lifted his head in a jerk, and with a smile that
was almost apologetic he brought her against him in a final
embrace. After an age he sighed softly, leaning back against
the door. 'Jane…I don't know what to say. You've made
your own life here. I've no right to intrude. But after tonight…'

She stared up at him, her hands lying against his chest.

'Marcus, I wish I could tell you I haven't changed, but it's no use pretending that either of us are the same people. But, yes, tonight was very special…it meant a great deal…'

'Then can we…I mean, when we will see each other again?'

'I…I don't know.' Her eyes sought his in the darkness. 'Marcus…I think we both need some sleep, don't you?'

His long fingers linked tightly into her own slender ones. 'I'm afraid that if I leave tonight, tomorrow things will be different.' He tilted her chin up in the moonlight, gazing down into her face. 'They won't be, will they?'

Jane stared into the intense grey eyes, aware that her life was indeed changing once more. Whether for better or worse she didn't know, only that she had no way of escaping and that even if she had, she probably wouldn't take it. Because of what she had done this evening, allowing him to make love to her, her resolve had weakened her fight to keep her defences in place, and she wanted him all over again with that desperate and urgent need he alone could fulfil. Wanted what she had missed for so many years, yearned for…the way he looked at her with those deep grey eyes as they made love, his lean and supple body next to her, those strong arms encircling her, his kiss and the way his lips lingered as though never wanting to leave.

'We'll talk about it tomorrow, if that's what you want…?' His question lingered in the air, and because she didn't answer he kissed her one last time, a kiss that made her ache impossibly for him as she watched him walk away to the car hidden in the shadows.

'I've had second thoughts about the hysterectomy,' Sue Porcher said quietly. 'You see, I think everyone should make an effort to find alternative cures…if you know what I mean, Dr Court.'

It was the following Tuesday and Jane sat back in her

chair, wondering what was going through her patient's mind. Was it her husband who had convinced her to abandon the hysterectomy? Clyde Oakman had mentioned that Brian Porcher had been depressed lately because of his wife's circumstances. But surely Brian wouldn't go as far as to persuade Sue that a son and heir was more important than her health?

'I accept that complementary medicine is there for us all to use, Sue,' Jane agreed, laying down her pen on the desk, 'but you've consulted one of the top specialists and he's told you that you need a hysterectomy. What's happened to change your mind?'

'Nothing,' Sue answered defensively. 'I just happen to think his decision wasn't the right one for me. I can handle the pain. The bleeding is a bit of a nuisance, but I'm taking a herbal remedy that Brian was recommended by a friend. His wife had difficult periods and it cleared the trouble up completely.'

'But it's not your periods that are the problem,' Jane pointed out. 'You've had gynae problems since Natasha was born. You've seen several specialists, both agreeing on the same treatment.'

'But I haven't consulted any alternative doctors,' Sue protested anxiously. 'I never gave it a thought till Bri—' She stopped, looking up at Jane. 'Well, until I sat down and really considered the future. I want a son. And I can't have one unless I have a womb. It's as simple as that.'

Jane sighed as she leaned forward. 'Sue, you have six lovely daughters. What if you have one more and it's a girl, too? Would you go on to try again?'

'I don't know,' Sue answered shortly. 'All I know is I've decided against an op and I thought it only fair to come in and tell you. But I didn't expect all this hassle. You've really surprised me, Dr Court. I thought you'd see my point of view.'

'I do,' Jane said as her patient stood up. 'It's because I'm concerned for you that I'm saying what I am.'

'Well, you needn't worry on my behalf, Dr Court. I feel much better already. And I've only been on this other treatment for a fortnight. I'm going to give it a chance and that's that.'

Before Jane could respond Sue picked up her bags and hurried from the room, almost bumping in to Annie in the corridor.

'Oh, Mrs Porcher—' Annie began, then stopped to stare after the departing figure.

'Come in, Annie,' Jane called, replacing Sue's notes in their folder.

Annie looked shocked as she entered. 'That's not like Mrs Porcher.'

'No, I agree,' Jane replied with a dismayed shrug. 'It was nothing to do with you, Annie.' Jane handed the notes to her. 'File them, please, Annie, and then I really would appreciate a cup of tea before I see Nancy Farlow.'

Annie nodded, placing the records on top of her paperwork. 'Yes, one coming up straight away, Dr Court. Your patient isn't here yet, but the nurse has set out the trolley in the treatment room and is ready and waiting.'

'OK. Thanks, Annie.'

Jane finally drank her cup of tea, but her thoughts were disturbed by Sue's attitude. It was clear the decision wasn't one she had come to on her own. Jane wondered if she should ring the Porchers and ask them to come in and see her. But what good would that do? Doubtless they would refuse her offer and she might only make matters worse.

She was concerned for her patient but she was also aware she had to accept the frustration of having to live with Sue's decision for the time being. Sue's desire for a son must be overwhelming and certainly Brian had had more to do with her reasoning than his wife had admitted. Did he realise that he was placing Sue's health in danger? He wasn't an unintelligent man. He had attended the consultations with Sue. He had to be aware of all the inherent dangers of her condition.

Jane sighed to herself as she finished her tea and as always these days her thoughts turned to Marcus and Ben and how, unlike Sue, she herself had never desired a baby in such a way. Her career had always come first after leaving London—part of her survival plan, she acknowledged, for the loss of Marcus. But she *had* agreed to take care of Ben in the event of Katrina's death, and a tiny ripple of pleasure floated over her skin as she recalled Ben as a baby. He had been so small, so vulnerable. Would she have been able to care for him as if he'd been her own?

The ripple of pleasure grew into a tide of warmth as Jane recalled Ben's small arms around her. A part of her entirely sympathised with the Porchers. It might seem that six healthy daughters were all that a husband and wife could ever want. But a son was something else...

Jane was shocked to find how disappointed she was when, on Friday Cenna fell victim to a virus, unable to get into work. Jean Thomas asked if it was possible for her to swap call duties with Cenna and, despite wanting to see Marcus and Ben, Jane felt obliged to agree.

It was the following week therefore, before they were able to meet, and she felt as though she had been separated from Marcus for a lifetime rather than two weeks. Seeing him at work only accentuated the loneliness and made more precious the few minutes they were able to spend together. By the time Saturday arrived she had almost convinced herself that something would happen to stop them from meeting.

When she looked through the kitchen window and saw Ben jump out of Marcus's car and run to the door, she tried to keep calm and collected. But Ben's excitement was infectious and she hugged him against her, listening with amusement to the gabbled flow of chatter.

'Sorry about that,' Marcus apologised, as they watched Ben run through to the garden. 'He couldn't wait to get here. Talked all the way over about you—' Marcus stopped, glancing over her shoulder. He pulled her into his arms, his mouth coming down on hers with an unexpected need. 'Oh, God, Jane, I needed that,' he breathed, hugging her against him.

She closed her eyes, frightened to confess how much she needed him, too. He kissed her again, his tongue seeking her response with an intensity that made her tremble. When Ben's voice came floating in, he grudgingly held her away. 'I don't know how I'm going to keep my hands off you,' he growled, just as Ben came bouncing into the lounge.

'Dr Court, Donovan's found a hole in the net. He's playing with the fish.'

Jane grinned, catching Marcus's eye as she held out her hand and Ben took hold of it. 'Ben, I think it's about time you started to call me Jane.'

Ben glanced at his father and Marcus nodded, a rueful smile spreading over his lips as Jane allowed herself to be tugged out to the garden.

'See?' Ben pointed to the evidence as Donovan groomed his wet paw. 'Do you think he caught one and ate it?'

'I don't think so.' Jane laughed. 'But we'd better check all the same. There should be six, so we'll count them, shall we?'

They spent some while in the garden, confirming the lively existence of all six fish and Donovan's innocence. Then, taking the picnic she had prepared, they set out for the beach. It was a warm June day, with a gentle breeze blowing in from the sea, and Jane made sure they were all smothered in sunscreen.

After driving along the coast they found a pretty cove sheltered by rocky cliffs. Ben ran down to the water while Marcus set up the wind-breaker. Jane had worn sporty blue Bermudas, a white T-shirt and a floppy straw hat, and as she stood watching Ben play in his trunks at the water's edge she recalled the day she had seen him with Mrs Barnes by the sea.

'Penny for your thoughts,' a voice said in her ear, and a hand snaked around her waist. Marcus stood at her side, his tall, bronzed frame clad in nothing but a pair of black shorts. She could feel the warmth of his body against her, the springy whorls of dark chest hair momentarily grazing her arm as he pulled her close.

She smiled, glancing up into his eyes. 'Oh, nothing very important.'

'You're not sorry you came?'

She looked up at him in surprise. 'No, of course not. I was just thinking when I first came for a swim this year...it seems ages ago now. I saw Ben with Mrs Barnes and another woman...I think it was probably her daughter. I watched them for a while. Ben was so happy playing in the water. I—I thought how much he looked like his mother.'

Marcus pulled her gently against him, his hand lying lightly on her waist. 'He does sometimes, doesn't he?'

She lifted her eyes slowly. 'Katrina was so small and—'

'Vulnerable?' Marcus offered, his expression unfathomable. 'Yes, she was.'

Suddenly the silence was broken by the screeching of gulls, and Ben squealed with delight as the birds swooped and soared above them, one of them diving down into the water and disappearing below the surface.

'Come on, let's see how warm the water is.' Marcus grabbed her hand and they ran into the sea to join Ben. As they played and paddled together, she told herself that now was not the time to bring up the past. Despite her attempts to fight her feelings for Marcus, it was clear to her that she had lost the battle. All she could hope to do now was to enjoy the day while she could.

Deciding to change her clothes before she was entirely soaked, she hurried back to the wind-breaker, managing to put all thoughts of Katrina from her mind. Changing into her pink and white bikini, she noticed that the two-piece had already allowed the sun to tan her skin a soft golden honey. As she approached the water's edge, Marcus's eyes went over her in a long, hungry stare and he waded towards her, the water running down his tanned, muscular limbs.

A thrill of excitement went through her and once again she found herself thinking how little changed he was. If anything, his physique was more stunning than ever. He grabbed her hand again and tugged her into the water as Ben threw them a bright red beach ball.

Dragging her eyes from Marcus's athletic body, Jane gave all her concentration to the game, finally collapsing beside Ben at the water's edge. Marcus swam out into the white crested waves, his dark head disappearing into the surf.

'Dad taught me to swim,' Ben chattered as they dug into the wet sand and made a sandcastle. He stopped for a moment, frowning up at her thoughtfully. 'Dad said you knew my mum…'

Jane patted the sand into place and lifted her eyes slowly. 'Yes, I did, Ben. We were friends, training to be doctors. And…and we shared a flat together.'

'Were you best friends?'

Jane nodded. 'Yes, we were, Ben.'

The boy pushed a sandy hand through his tousled hair and sniffed. 'I've got a best friend, too. His name's Darren. He lives in the next road so he can come round after school. Mrs Barnes lets us play in her garden.'

'I think it's important to have a good friend.' Jane smiled

as she watched the sea fill the little moat around their sand-castle.

'That's why I don't want to move from Nair,' Ben murmured, his beautiful dark eyes making it impossible for Jane not to see Katrina in their depths. 'I hope Dad says we don't have to leave.'

Jane felt a pang of dismay as she looked at Ben. What could she say to him? In just a few weeks she had become used to their presence in her life. But she hadn't allowed herself to think ahead or to question the arrangement that had been made in the first instance. If Marcus was to have second thoughts about staying, then surely he would say? Even Phillip had pressed him about staying on and the answer had been firmly in the negative.

'Are you hungry?' Jane changed the subject tactfully and nodded to the distant figure now swimming towards them. 'Your father's going to be ravenous after that swim. Let's go and see what we can find for lunch.'

Ben jumped to his feet and once again Jane felt his small fingers slide through hers. When they arrived at the wind-breaker, Jane spread out two large blankets and covered the picnic hamper with a cloth.

As Ben helped her set out the food, she brought her mind firmly back to the present. She wasn't going to brood over the past or the future. Today was what was important and she was going to enjoy every precious minute of it.

The afternoon was overcast but warm and they swam and played in the water until the beach was deserted. Eventually they cleared up the picnic things and dressed in warmer clothes to ward off the evening breeze. Then they returned to the car and drove home.

By the time they reached Nair it was almost dark and Ben had fallen asleep on the back seat. 'Will you come in for a drink?' Jane asked as Marcus switched off the engine.

'I think he's out for the count.' Marcus shrugged as he turned and they gazed down at the sleeping child. 'I'd better get him home, showered and into bed.'

'It's been a wonderful day,' Jane whispered, not wanting it to end.

Marcus reached across and took her hand. 'You've made it very special.'

'He's a lovely boy, Marcus. So easy to be with.'

Marcus grinned. 'Like his father, I hope.'

Jane smiled. 'Stop fishing for compliments.'

Marcus leaned towards her, his voice low and husky. 'I want more than compliments. I want you, Dr Court...all of you. In my arms, in my bed...in—'

'Shh...' Jane laid her fingers over his lips as she glanced down at Ben.

'When can I see you again?' Marcus lifted one dark eyebrow. 'Tomorrow?'

Once again indecision filled her. Her better judgement, the sound voice of reason deep inside her, told her she must protect herself from further heartbreak, and she knew that voice spoke the truth.

She had spent long years trying to get over Marcus and now seeing him again so consistently had reopened the locked memories that had once caused so much pain and indeed, years before, so much happiness. Marcus and Ben were far from being permanent fixtures in her life. Only a fool would have contested that fact.

No matter how hard she tried to fight her feelings, in her heart had she always known the struggle was a wasted effort? Was she really prepared to accept a few months of happiness before Marcus's contract ended? How she wished she was strong enough to stop now, while she had the chance. It wasn't too late—or was it?

'Ben's going out for the afternoon with his friend Darren,' Marcus was saying as he took her chin in his fingers and lifted her face so that she was forced to look into his eyes. 'Darren's parents are taking them to the aquatic centre at Bournemouth. Could I interest you in a drive out somewhere?'

Desperately she sought for an excuse as the thoughts battled in her head, one part of her desperate to agree, the other uttering that warning which she had tried so hard to heed.

'I'll take that as a yes,' he whispered and, covering her lips with a passionate kiss, she knew that she had never had any real chance of protecting herself. From the first moment he'd walked back into her room at the surgery, she'd known she'd never stopped loving him...never.

He finally released her and it was on shaking legs that she climbed out of the car. Marcus accompanied her to the front door with the hamper, and his warm body moved against her, his hand pulling her urgently towards him. 'I'll miss you,' he whispered, and kissed her again, this time his lips parting hers with an urgent need she couldn't resist.

Conscious of Ben asleep in the car, she finally moved away, her eyes telling him all he wanted to know. As the car moved off she closed the front door and stood in her small hallway, his kiss still burning on her lips.

As the moon shone through the window and spilled silver light across the floor she sighed, giving herself up to the inevitable. Tomorrow seemed a long way away.

It was late morning when Marcus arrived, and Jane opened the door to the sight of a large bouquet, a vivid array of summer flowers that held her spellbound. Marcus looked somewhat abashed. 'I didn't think chocolates would appeal at this time of the morning.' He grinned.

Once inside, he followed her to the kitchen. Jane filled the vase and arranged the flowers. 'They're beautiful, Marcus—'

'But nowhere near as beautiful as you,' he interrupted huskily, turning her around to face him. She looked up into his face, her hands slipping to his shoulders, the thin material of his dark blue T-shirt soft against her fingers. Underneath, the muscle moved, hard and sinewy. It all came back to her then, a sensation of physical strength and intimacy. Everything about him was so familiar and the passion flowing between them felt unstoppable.

His fingers tangled in her hair and massaged the hollow at the back of her neck, sending shivers down her spine. Wearing only a thin shift dress, she felt her body shudder as his hands travelled downwards over her hips to bring her hard against him.

'Has…has Ben gone with Darren?' she managed to whisper as his lips closed over her mouth.

The abrupt nod he gave in answer left her in no doubt they had several hours ahead of them and, taking his hand, she led him through the kitchen and up the stairs to the bedroom. For a moment he raised her chin and gazed into her eyes, his tender, sexy smile reminding her so vividly of the young Marcus so many years ago. But then the passion of his kiss made her forget the past and they slipped into a world of their own, his arms holding her tightly, urgently.

'Oh, Jane, you've no idea how much I need you…'

'As much as I need you,' she murmured as she pulled at his T-shirt, prising it from the belt at his waist and helping him to pull it over his head.

Their fingers were trembling with the effort and she was hardly aware of her accelerated breathing. As he slid the straps of her dress from her shoulders, she eased the material down over her body. He gave a small gasp as he stared at her, his grey eyes hungrily moving over her body.

Inside her there was an ache that longed to be released as he touched her. It was as though he had never seen her before, his fingers tracing a slow path over her bra and panties, softly caressing her thighs. She thought she would scream if he didn't stop and take her into his arms. At the point where she could bear it no longer, he seemed to recognise her need. With a swift, powerful sweep of his arms he lifted her up and onto the bed.

Moments later they were lying alongside one another, their clothes abandoned on the floor. The hardness of his body left her in no doubt that his need was as great as hers, and with a willing abandon she gave herself up to him. Once again they were lovers. Sex between them had always been wonderful and nothing had changed. Their passion was totally fulfilling and, with each other's needs satisfied, their pent-up desire exploded in one final act of fulfilment.

Finally she lay still and at peace in his arms, their bodies damp with sweat, the bedclothes tangled around them. Marcus's fingers stoked through her hair as her head nestled on his shoulder. His breathing was slow and rhythmic and she knew he was falling asleep. Minutes later, curled beside him, she also fell asleep, her body and spirit utterly and completely fulfilled.

CHAPTER NINE

OVER the next few weeks Jane and Marcus found time for one another, sometimes snatching small breaks at lunchtime, occasionally in the evenings, but the happiest times were shared with Ben. Their outings to the beach and countryside became events to look forward to, and Jane found it increasingly easy to talk to him, sharing small memories and the happier recollections of the past.

The new surgery was well on its way to completion when, one early July day, Jane found herself alone with Phil at the town centre site. Three floors high and rendered in a modern, decorative pale brick, the red-tiled roof looked almost opulent in the hot sunshine.

'The extension was the most problematic of all, as you know,' Phil was telling Jane as they walked slowly around the exterior. 'But the foundations are going down this week. Another couple of months and we should see the whole building *in situ*.'

'The place is very impressive,' Jane said admiringly as they stood with several other onlookers, admiring the building. 'But sometimes I just can't believe we'll really be moving. In some ways I feel quite sad about leaving the old place.'

'I know what you mean,' Phil agreed quietly. It was a very warm day and he stood in his white short-sleeved shirt and casual grey trousers. His dark brown eyes, thickly fringed with black lashes, regarded the new practice building thoughtfully. 'We've been very lucky. Old Nair Surgery has been a happy practice on the whole.'

124

Jane nodded, her blue eyes meeting Phil's. 'It has been for me. I couldn't have been happier anywhere.'

A strange expression crossed his face. 'You were unhappy when you joined us, weren't you, Jane?'

Warm colour filled her cheeks. 'Yes, but that was a long time ago.'

'Are you happy now?'

'Yes...I am, Phil.'

'So we won't...we won't be losing you...?'

Jane turned, looking up in surprise. 'What makes you ask that?'

Phil grinned sheepishly. 'I don't know really. I've had this odd feeling lately. You've been rather distant—I was wondering if I'd done anything to upset you.'

'Oh, Phil, of course you haven't.' Jane looked up into his anxious eyes. 'If I've seemed distant, I suppose it's because...because of something that happened...when—'

'You don't have to explain anything to me, Jane.' Phil gave a quick shrug, guiding her away from the new practice and leading her towards the cars parked on the vacant plot next door. 'All I hope is that the move isn't going to change things—I mean, we make a good team, don't we? And Cenna seems happy enough—we only need one good partner to complete the equation.'

Jane paused as she came to her car. The sun reflected brightly off the bonnet and she raised her hand to shield the reflection from her eyes. 'And you were hoping it might be Marcus?'

Again Phil gave a brief shrug. 'Yes, I had hoped that, but it doesn't seem very likely. And, strangely, you don't seem to be much in favour of the idea either.'

'Phil, I...I should have told you before...' Jane hesitated as she moved to stand in the shade. 'But there's never really been time—or the occasion. And to be honest, I had hoped I might never have to say anything. Phil, Marcus and I have known each other a long time.' She shook her head slowly, wondering how she could explain. 'We…we trained together in London.' She bit her lip and with a deep sigh added, 'And it was a little more than training together, much more, actually. We were planning to marry.'

'Oh, God…Jane—'

'Unhappily,' she rushed on as Phil stared incredulously at her, 'it didn't work out and Marcus married someone else.'

It was a while before Phil replied, his frown revealing the extent of his confusion. 'Jane, you should have said. And here's me, trying to persuade you that he's the right chap for the job.'

'That's the point, Phil,' Jane answered quickly. 'He probably is. Marcus is a brilliant doctor and perfect for the new practice. It's just bad luck that we happened to have quite a past history between us.'

'I wish you could have taken me into your confidence,' Phil said quietly. 'I would never have kept hinting the way I have.'

'Well, I hardly think it fair that the past comes into it…'

'Of course it does. You are my first concern, Jane.'

'You're very sweet, Phil, but you've had enough troubles of your own.'

His face, surrounded by a thatch of deep brown hair, suddenly darkened. 'Maggie's death hit me pretty hard, yes. But I'm coping. And the last thing I want to do is make things awkward for you.'

'You haven't. Marcus and I…have come to an understanding while he's working here.' Jane felt her face grow embarrassingly warm.

'Well, thank God for that,' Phil sighed, a smile of relief on his lips. 'But I promise you, from now on my lips are sealed. I understand that no way would you want a partnership with Marcus, even if he was to express a wish to stay in Nair, which is, I must add, about as unlikely as finding life on Mars. After his contract is finished here I think he may intend visiting his sister in Florida. He mentioned they were close and hadn't seen each other in some while. She's coming over to England for a short stay soon—did you know her?'

Jane nodded, recalling clearly Marcus's adopted sister. 'Yes…I know Sara. She's a little younger than Marcus and married with two young sons.'

'And a physiotherapist, I understand?'

Jane nodded. 'We all knew each other in London before Sara married.'

'An American?' Phil said and again Jane nodded.

'Greg Thompson. He's a lawyer…and met Sara whilst she was on holiday in Florida. Marcus and Sara's late parents lived out there when they retired.'

But she wasn't concentrating on her conversation with Phil. The fact she had to accept—that Marcus was leaving—was a fact she had tried hard to ignore over the weeks and months, convincing herself that she should enjoy the time they had left together. Neither had Marcus brought up the subject. To be fair, it had been her who had taken care to point out his contract was temporary, she rationalised.

'I must go, Phil,' she said quickly, suddenly unable to hide the dismay that Phil's comments had caused her. 'I've several more calls to make. See you back at surgery this afternoon?'

'Yes, yes, indeed. And…er…thanks for sharing things with me, Jane.'

'Sorry I left it so late.' She smiled at him, afraid to linger.

As she drove away, Phil was walking back into the area designated as the foundations for the extension which would house a mini-clinic for small operations. She felt she should have enthused more with Phil and felt a pang of guilt at her quick departure.

But her stomach felt filled with a lead weight, and as the thoughts flew around in her mind she tried not to panic. Marcus had brought Ben to Nair because of the temperate climate and sea air, and to a great extent his hopes had been fulfilled. Ben's asthma had improved. She had forced herself not to dwell on either the past or future, but to live for the day. And out of this had come the relationship she had formed with Ben and his improvement in health. If only for that, she should be glad.

But Jane was unable to console herself. She still loved Marcus and had never stopped loving him in all the years they had spent apart. So much about their relationship remained the same...better perhaps than it had been when they were younger. The years had deepened that passion, strengthened her need for him and now for Ben.

With a start, she realised she had reached Nair Surgery. She hardly recalled having made the journey, passing other traffic or pulling into the car park. Her mind had been in turmoil. All she knew as she brought the car to a halt was that she had been hurt before and was now hurting in the same way again. How could she have allowed herself to fall into the trap?

As she looked at herself in the driving mirror and saw two pools of shimmering blue gazing back at her, she accepted the inevitable. She had entered into their affair willingly and at times desperately. Her hunger had been insatiable. She had agreed to their love-making—at any price. She could only continue to love Marcus and to love Ben. And what was worse, she couldn't stop that love, not even if her life depended on it.

'Mr Macauley is being transferred to a rehabilitation unit,' Paula said one morning a few days later as Jane walked into the office. Paula lowered the telephone, covering the mouthpiece with her hand. 'He's asked the social worker

to personally let you know.' The receptionist gave a wry
smile as she raised her eyebrows. 'I think he's worried he
won't be getting any more oranges.'

Jane smiled as she walked to the office desk and peered
down at the address written on the pad. 'Pass the message
on that I'll see him soon, Paula.'

As Paula resumed her conversation, Jane noted that the
unit was closer to Nair than Southampton. As soon as she
found a spare hour she would drive there. The second visit
she'd made to see Mr Macauley had resulted in an approv-
ing smile as she'd presented him with a basket of fruit, and
a modicum of reasonable conversation had transpired.

She had also discovered that Timothy Lister was a regular visitor to the elderly man. When she had passed
Timothy's thanks to Marcus she hadn't realised that, but
the irony wasn't lost on her when one of the medical team
had disclosed the fact.

'I don't envy the poor soul who has to rehabilitate Mr
M.,' Paula said as she replaced the phone. 'You know, I've
known him ever since I started to work here ten years ago.
And I don't think I've ever got a smile out of him. He must
have a soft spot for you.'

'I very much doubt it.' Jane laughed.

'Well, whatever your charms, you've got a fan club
there.'

'Only as long as the freebies continue.' Jane chuckled
then, frowning at Paula, she added, 'Is it really ten years
you've worked here?'

Paula nodded, sighing softly. 'I was nineteen when I
started with Dr Jardine. He'd just taken over from his father.' Then she grinned. 'I'll be sorry to move, you know.
I've a lot of happy memories of this old place.'
Momentarily her smile faded. 'John used to pick me up in
his old banger after work before we were married. On summer evenings we'd drive down to the beach and swim.

They were the best days, really free. You know, the only regret I have after John's death is that we spent so much time apart. The sea took up too much of our lives.'

Jane saw the sadness briefly fill Paula's eyes. The drowning of her fisherman husband two years ago hadn't prevented Paula from continuing bravely, working hard to support their two children. Jane admired the young woman and knew that she had sympathised deeply with Phil's grief when Maggie had died.

'It must still hurt to have lost him so young,' Jane said quietly.

'Yes. It does. But time's flown,' Paula said quickly, regaining her composure. 'And life gets busier by the moment, doesn't it, Dr Court? That's why you should find more time for yourself, you know. Life is for enjoying as well as working hard. Now, before I forget, Dr Granger asked me to give you this note. He had to go out or he would have given it to you himself.' Paula passed her a small white envelope.

'Thanks, Paula. I'll be in my room if you want me.' Jane slid the note into her pocket and, glancing at her watch, saw that she had ten minutes before her morning surgery began. Sitting at her desk, she opened the letter.

Her heart raced as she read Marcus's even hand, her hands trembling slightly as her eyes flew over the words.

'Darling, I've a visitor arriving—Sara, in fact. She's staying in Nair for a fortnight. Mrs Barnes has found her a room and insists we have tea in the garden this evening. Come and join us. Love, M.'

As Nancy Farlow entered as her first patient, Jane slid the note into her pocket, deciding that to meet Sara again would be more than she could bear. She had liked Sara a lot, and as a couple she and Marcus had often spent time with Sara and her husband Greg. To talk about those times, as they inevitably would, could only mean painful memories resurfacing. And despite the fact that she'd lost the battle to protect herself from further heartbreak as far as the future went, she could at least avoid the pain of recalling the past.

So by the time Nancy sat down Jane had decided not to accept Marcus's invitation, and she brought her thoughts back firmly to the present.

'I've been told at the hospital I have something called...' Nancy Farlow read from a scrap of paper, '"Actinic keratosis". What in heaven's name is that?'

'Actinic keratosis,' replied Jane carefully, 'is a condition of the skin causing a roughness and thickening. This is usually due to overexposure to solar radiation which is especially likely to occur near the sea in summer or from snow in winter.'

'That's all I need,' Nancy sighed. 'I can't even wear my make-up now. Look at this.' She turned her head to one side and indicated the unpleasantly inflamed side of her face. 'I'm in a real mess. The cryosurgery seems to make the lesions worse. I'm going to look like Frankenstein's bride.'

'I'm sure that won't be the case,' Jane answered quickly as she stood up and, bending over her patient, examined the inflamed areas. 'You know, there's very little scarring left after cryosurgery, very often just small white patches.'

'So you really think it's worth me persisting?' Nancy asked as Jane returned to her chair. 'I'm beginning to have my doubts.'

'Certainly it's worth persisting.' Jane paused. 'Have you found a job yet?'

'Looking like this?' Nancy raised an eyebrow. 'Part of my job in PR is to look presentable. Clients would run a mile if they could see me now!'

'So...what are you doing with yourself these days?'

Nancy Farlow's vivid blue eyes hadn't lost their glint of

amusement. 'I'm sculpting. Used to sculpt for a hobby years ago, so I figured I'd have to do something to while away the time. I've even sold a few pieces.'

'What do you sculpt?' Jane asked curiously.

'Abstracts mostly.'

'Well, I envy your talent.' Jane sighed ruefully. 'I wouldn't know where to begin.'

'When you're desperate, you soon apply yourself,' Nancy said as she rose to her feet.

Jane nodded and said with a smile, 'Meanwhile, keep those outpatient appointments, won't you?'

Nancy shrugged as she opened the door. 'If you say so, Doc. But I've no idea how it's all going to end.'

It was a sentiment that Jane could sympathise with as she thought of her own circumstances. A deep ache filled her as her mind flashed up images of the last time Marcus had made love to her at the cottage. She recalled every movement, every whispered word. She could feel him now, hard and strong against her, taste his kiss as his hands explored her with an intensity that left her breathless.

Reaching into her pocket, Jane drew out the note and read it once more. Almost before finishing it, she knew that it was hopeless. She had no self-control where Marcus was concerned. She wanted to be with him…ached to be with him…no matter where he was or who he was with.

The last patient left her room at just after five and Jane signed the last few prescriptions, handing them to Paula as she left. It was twenty minutes later when she drove home and unlocked the front door. Ten minutes later she had changed into shorts and a casual shirt, her intention being to take her tea into the garden and sit on the patio.

But as she gazed out onto the street, a bright green Space Cruiser pulled into the kerb. She was shocked to see Ben and Darren sitting in the rear while Marcus emerged from the passenger side.

As she opened the front door, Ben was clambering down from the vehicle and ran towards her. 'Jane, my Aunt Sara is here,' he shouted excitedly. 'She lives in America, but she's come here for a holiday.' Ben grabbed Jane's hand and Darren joined them, a small boy with freckles and fair hair who had become a regular visitor to Hillcrest.

'Hello, Darren. Well…this is a surprise.' Jane looked up to meet Marcus's grey gaze. The evening was warm and mellow and Marcus was wearing shorts and a T-shirt, his feet clad in thongs.

'Jane…? You didn't arrive. I thought perhaps you didn't get my message.' His expression was concerned, and as she opened the door wider she caught sight of the figure behind him. Jane recalled Sara as a vivacious, dark-haired girl in her early twenties. Now Sara had matured into an attractive woman, her ebony hair pulled back from her face and her grey eyes, so like her brother's, shining warmly as she moved forward to embrace Jane.

'After all this time—it's so good to see you again,' Sara said in her warm and friendly American accent. 'I hope we haven't called when you're busy?'

'Not at all,' Jane responded at once. 'I…er…didn't manage to leave early this afternoon,' she added by way of rather a lame apology. 'Come through—the boys have already gone into the garden.'

The ice was soon broken as Jane made tea and soft drinks for the boys, and her fears that the past might dominate the conversation proved groundless as Sara chatted to them about her children—Ben's cousins—and the holiday they had taken in order to visit Greg's parents.

'I hope you've not changed your mind about coming over to see us when your contract is finished, Marcus,' Sara said eventually as they finished their tea.

Throwing a glance at his sister, Marcus nodded. 'No, I haven't,' he answered abruptly.

'We could take the boys to Disneyland,' Sara went on to suggest. 'I think you would enjoy it. The last time we visited I couldn't drag Greg away.' She added as she leaned forward, 'But the fall is a long way off. In the meantime it would be wonderful if Ben could come back with me to Cornwall and meet his uncle and cousins.'

Marcus was silent for a moment, then shrugged. 'I'm sure he'd like that. My only concern is his asthma...though I have to say recently it hasn't been troublesome.'

'Then why don't you come back with us?' Sara suggested easily. 'At least for a few days.' Then turning to Jane she added, 'And Jane, too?'

The pressure of work at the height of the season made it out of the question to think of accepting Sara's invitation. Despite Marcus's entreaty that they could manage at least a weekend away, Jane remained firm in her refusal.

It wasn't that she didn't want to be with Marcus and Ben, quite the reverse. She could think of nothing she would have liked better, but she was also aware that if she agreed to the trip, it would only create more intimacy between the three of them. For Ben's sake alone, she felt she had to draw a boundary somewhere, and with surgeries extended to accommodate a rush of temporary residents it seemed timely that she should do so here.

In the end, Marcus agreed to going away to Cornwall for a week. Phil suggested they do a swap since Phil had plans for a week's sailing later in the summer and, with pressure from Sara and Ben to accept, the dates were finally confirmed.

On the Saturday they were due to leave for Cornwall, Jane promised Ben and Marcus she would drive up to Hillcrest to say goodbye. It was very warm in the cottage and she put on a cool cotton shift in a summery peach colour, slipping on low-heeled sandals and scooping her blonde hair into a clip.

As she drove up to the Westcliffe, a misty sun broke through the haze and the sweep of sea to her right glistened magnificently like a calm silver pond. Early morning gulls scavenging along the cliffs cried noisily, while the first tourists hurried down to the beach.

At Hillcrest, Sara, dressed in jeans and a sweatshirt, hurried across the lawn to say goodbye, giving Jane a hug as she climbed out of her car. Marcus, clad similarly in T-shirt and shorts, was stowing the luggage in the Space Cruiser. As he turned to lift two large cases into the boot of his own car he caught sight of her, and her heart missed a beat as it never failed to do when she saw him.

Suddenly Ben, in a bright red T-shirt, ran from the house and there was a mixture of excitement and apprehension in his eyes as he hugged her.

'You'll send me a card, won't you?' she whispered in his ear—an ear smelling of the achingly personal aroma that was Ben. It was a fragrance linked to Marcus, a hint of the cologne he always used added to the soapy, newly washed smell that Ben carried with him, too.

'Aunt Sara says I can phone you,' Ben answered, his slender arms firmly entwined about her neck. There was a hitch in his voice and Jane hugged him a little tighter, her eyes for one moment misting as the poignant moment made her even more certain she had done right in refusing Sara's invitation.

'Have you remembered your sunglasses?' she asked, quickly regaining her composure.

Ben nodded, drawing them from his shorts' pocket and sliding them up his nose. They were still spattered with white emulsion and they both laughed.

'Have a lovely time with your cousins.' Jane prised him

gently away from her. 'When you come home Donovan and I will want to know all about Cornwall.'

'I wish you were coming with us.'

Finding a bright smile from somewhere, she said cheerfully, 'Me, too.'

'Aunt Sara's got a dog.' Ben pushed the sunglasses onto the top of his head, obviously attempting delay tactics. 'But I like cats best.'

'Come along, young man,' Marcus called, beckoning his son. 'Time to go.'

'Bye, Jane.' Unexpectedly Ben stood on tiptoe and planted a kiss on her cheek, before climbing in the Space Cruiser beside his aunt.

Finally Marcus walked towards her and for a moment their eyes met. 'It's going to be a long week,' he said quietly, and she nodded, struggling with the conflicting emotions inside her. She wanted to draw him against her and tell him she loved him and would miss him, but she merely lifted her face to his kiss. His lips softly swept across her cheek and their gentle embrace left her longing desperately for the warmth of his arms and the feel of his strong body against her.

'Ben is really looking forward to this,' she said, her voice sounding unnaturally light. 'Have a wonderful time.'

'I know,' he told her huskily. 'But that won't stop me missing you.'

And as they parted an ache deep inside her grew out of all proportion as she watched the two vehicles move off, knowing that the days would seem endless while they were gone.

CHAPTER TEN

CENNA completed her morning's paperwork, noting the latest report from the rehabilitation unit where Frederick Macauley was convalescing. She pondered for a moment on the remarks that his social worker had made. Should she ring the social worker's extension number? But there was little she could add to the conclusion the various departments had arrived at—Frederick Macauley was too infirm to return to his home and the outlook for his future did not seem good.

She pushed back the wing of dark hair that had fallen across her face and gazed out through her window, her attention caught by the tall, slim figure of Jane walking into the surgery.

Jane saw her and, tapping her arm, indicated her watch. Cenna nodded, rising from her chair. A few minutes later Jane entered the room, her blonde eyebrows arched. 'Have you a few moments to spare, Cenna?'

'Yes—as a matter of fact I wanted to speak to you, too. Sit down and I'll ask Annie to bring us some coffee.'

Jane sat down with a long sigh. 'Coffee sounds great. I've ten minutes or so before I start my surgery—what about you?'

'Yes, me, too.' Cenna lifted the phone and a few minutes later was deep into a discussion with Jane over the problem of Frederick Macauley's future. By the time Annie brought coffee for them, Cenna had explained that neither the unit nor the social services were happy about the pensioner returning home.

'There are two options,' Cenna explained as she handed

Jane the letter. 'Residential care or sheltered housing, and I don't think the latter would be suitable. Mr Macauley is only mobile with the aid of a Zimmer and he's very frail, as you know.'

Jane nodded thoughtfully. 'I haven't yet visited him at the unit, although when I saw him in hospital it was early days.'

'I'm afraid the news isn't good. As his GP, and bearing in mind the events of the last year, residential care would be preferable. There's no family to help and going home to that large house of his would be courting disaster.'

'He's going to put up a fight,' Jane mused. 'He's very independent.'

'But not able to look after himself now,' Cenna pointed out. 'Apart from the impaired vision and hearing, he's had the hip operation to contend with and the hernia. I'd like to speak to him as his GP, but I don't think he would be too receptive. However, he's taken a shine to you—'

'And you'd like me to broach the subject?' Jane interrupted with a wry smile.

'Would you mind?'

'No, although I don't know how far I'll get. But I'll try.'

'The authorities have made suggestions—you might like to speak to the social worker beforehand,' Cenna commented. Sipping her coffee pensively, she added, 'Have you heard from Marcus?'

Jane nodded as she met Cenna's enquiring gaze. 'Yes, he's phoned several times, and Ben, too. They seem to be having great fun.'

Cenna noted her friend's hesitation and guessed how much she must be missing them. As Jane sat back in the chair, she gave a rueful smile.

'I know what you're thinking, Cenna—and, yes, this has seemed rather a long week without them about the place.'

Tilting her head to one side, she added, 'You don't seem surprised.'

It was Cenna's turn to smile as she saw Jane's candid expression. 'No, I'm not surprised but I'm also…a little concerned—for you.'

After a pause, Jane asked, 'You think it's reckless of me to have an affair with Marcus when I know he's leaving?'

'I just hope,' Cenna said quickly, her amber eyes meeting Jane's, 'that you won't be hurt again.'

Jane looked down at her hands, her blonde hair falling over her face. 'Which is one reason I chose not to go to Cornwall. Of course, I wanted to, but…well, let's just say my sensible side knew it would be wrong.' After a while, Jane looked up, a smile once again on her face. 'I'll see Mr Macauley for you and see what I can do.'

After Jane had left the room Cenna felt a deep pang of sympathy for her friend, but there seemed no solution to the problem. She only had to reflect on the emotional tangle she herself was in to know she couldn't help.

Cenna was certain that Phil had no idea of the way she felt about him—she hardly knew herself, hardly dared think, let alone put the emotion into words. She only knew that when Phil was near her she felt whole—complete—an emotion which she suspected Jane felt about Marcus and Ben as well which, in the circumstances, was heartbreaking.

It was a hot, slightly overcast day when Jane set off to see Frederick Macauley. The rehabilitation unit wasn't far from Nair and the small reception area was busy with visitors. Waiting her turn, Jane finally asked for directions through the sprawling building. She made her way along the busy corridors, only to discover that Mr Macauley wasn't in the visitors' lounge, as first thought, but in his own room.

When she arrived there, the elderly man was lying on his bed, his Zimmer to one side. As the door was open, she walked in, knocking first then entering as the elderly man beckoned to her.

Jane was shocked to witness his loss of weight. After telling him who she was, she took the chair he gestured to and set the basket of fruit she had brought with her on the side table.

'S'pose they told you I'm not fit enough to go home,' Frederick Macauley said in a tired voice.

'How do you feel about that?' Jane asked quietly, dismayed to see that he showed no interest in the fruit.

'Been feeling a bit tired lately. All these damn exercises they keep making me do.'

'Dr Lloyd asked me to pass on her regards,' Jane said, intending to change the subject, but she needn't have worried for slowly he drifted into sleep, despite the noise of the visitors in the corridor outside.

She sat for some while and then, realising someone was standing in the doorway, she turned. Timothy Lister, dressed in jeans and a denim jacket and leaning on a walking aid, nodded to her.

'How are you?' she asked in surprise as she rose and walked to the door.

'Much better, thanks. Having forty winks, is he?'

Jane smiled as she glanced back at the bed. 'I think he'd prefer a siesta rather than having to talk to me.'

'He'll like the fruit.' Timothy grinned. 'Usually takes his teeth out to eat the bananas.'

'Usually?'

'I come to see him a fair bit. He doesn't get many visitors. Like you said in hospital, he's not used to people. But we've struck up a bit of a friendship. S'pose being in hospital together helps.' The young man looked at Jane with a frown. 'He won't be going home, so I understand?'

Jane shook her head slowly. 'It's doubtful.'

'I didn't think so.'

They stood for a while in silence, Frederick Macauley's shallow breathing the only noise to break the silence. Then quietly they left the room and walked slowly along the corridor. When they took leave of each other at Reception, Jane had discovered that Timothy—ironically enough— was the old man's only visitor, apart from herself, and on the way home she pondered on the mysteries of Mother Nature.

Mr Macauley had won himself the friendship of a young man who had been involved in an accident which had occurred indirectly because of Mr Macauley himself. If it hadn't been for Timothy, his stay at the rehabilitation unit would have been a very lonely one.

The days seemed to drag by until Marcus came home, and it was with a fast-beating heart that she opened the door to him on Sunday morning.

Once inside the cottage Marcus slid his hand around her waist and pulled her against him, no words necessary as they fell into each other's arms. The balm of desire that made everything right again filled Jane as she closed her eyes and gave herself up to the kisses that she had waited so long for and had missed so deeply. At last he broke away, his eyes full of the passion that flared between them.

'That was quite some hello,' Marcus whispered as for a long while they held each other, almost afraid to move. Then, without words, he took her hand and led her into the garden and toward the swing seat.

Words between them came slowly, grudgingly, as though all they said was a mere formality, a prelude to their one wish, to be close to one another, to make love. When he'd told her about Ben and she'd given a brief summary of what had happened at work, he took her into his arms and crushed her against him.

'Jane, oh, Jane, how I've longed to hold you,' he

growled, seeking her mouth with hard, demanding kisses that didn't stop until she was breathless, marvelling anew at her need for him.

'Do you mind,' he asked in a low and ragged voice, 'if I totally monopolise you for the next few hours?'

She found herself laughing at the absurdity of his question as the soft breeze drifted around them, the silence somehow making the moment very special. Then the early morning sun began to shed its warm rays into the garden and a heady mixture of mown lawns and sea salt filled the air.

Marcus kissed her again and she felt the heat of his body under the white T-shirt and navy shorts, felt his thigh burning against her dress, the hard maleness of his body sending little shivers down her spine.

He always had that effect on her; she only had to look into his eyes to be transported into another world, and this morning was no exception. When his lips burned over hers, she slid her arms around his neck, feeling the warm, strong muscles move under her fingertips as he scooped her up and into his arms.

Marcus's chest rose rhythmically under Jane's cheek. They had made love without the pressure of time against them, and her fulfilment was complete. His hand rested on her hair, inquisitive fingers softly playing with the silky strands.

'Are you asleep?' he asked softly.

'No.' She snuggled into him, feeling his hard, lean body against her. 'Do you have to leave?'

He pulled her against him, his fingers running over the curve of her hip and trailing softly over her arm. 'Mrs Barnes has been very discreet and resisted asking any questions. As long as you've no objection to me staying…?'

'Now, that's another silly question,' she whispered as she lifted her face to his kiss.

His lips closed over hers, returning her senses to chaos as he pulled her against him. Lifting her into his arms, she melted against him, feeling his arousal and barely containing her own excitement. The moments seemed to go on for ever as he teased and caressed her, occasionally pausing and staring at her nakedness. Then in one frantic movement of desire she was beneath him once more, their bodies finding a new rhythm, a completeness.

As her heart raced and her mind cut off from the real world, she gave all of herself to him, crying aloud as his breath stilled, his body tensed like a bow above her.

'Jane…' he groaned raggedly, and his voice lingered in her brain as they clung together, hopelessly lost in the world of their passion.

Later he slid beside her, breathless and shuddering, and she took him in her arms. She lifted one hand slowly, unable to speak, stroking the damp, black hair that had fallen over his forehead. Raising herself against his body, she slithered down to join him between the tangled sheets.

His strong arms pulled her against his chest and she breathed slowly against the wiry curls of thick dark hair. There was no need for words and she laid her head in the crook of his arm and together they fell asleep.

It was a windy but hot August Wednesday and the surgery was full of summer ills—coughs and colds and overexposure to the previous few days of hot sun.

But it was none of these minor ailments that Sue Porcher complained of as she entered Jane's room with her husband Brian. Taking the chair by the desk, she sat down slowly, her pale face shadowed by a wing of dark brown hair.

Her husband stood at her side, his sturdy frame dressed in working clothes, a pair of well-worn overalls and T-shirt. 'We've got some good news,' he said quickly as his wife glanced at Jane. 'Sue's pregnant.'

Jane looked at her patient and paused. 'You're certain, Sue?'

'Well, that's why I'm here, to confirm it with you. But I'm pretty sure.'

'I see.' Once again Jane paused before she spoke. 'Well, let's have you up on the bench and—'

'The thing is,' Brian interrupted as his wife moved to stand up, 'this might be our last chance, seeing as how Sue's been told she needs a hysterectomy. So we're really counting on your support, Dr Court.'

'I'll do whatever I can to help, of course.' Jane glanced up at the big fisherman.

'But you're not all for it, are you?' Brian asked quickly.

'The decision to have another child is entirely up to you and Sue,' Jane responded as she rose to her feet. 'You have all the information we could give you. And Sue has seen two consultants over the past few months. Besides which, isn't what I think a little beside the point now that Sue is pregnant?'

Brian laughed as his wife rose to her feet. 'Well, we had to jump one way or t'other. Time's rolling on, as they say.'

'I'll be out in a minute, Brian,' Sue Porcher said quickly, giving her husband a gentle push to the door. 'You've done your bit, now I'll do mine.'

The big man grinned and, saying goodbye, left the room. When Jane helped her patient on the bench and began to examine her, Sue spoke candidly.

'This really is the last one, Dr Court. After this baby, I'll have the hysterectomy.'

'And what if it's a girl and not a boy?' Jane asked as she gently palpated Sue's abdomen. 'You won't be able to send her back.'

'Well, at least I'll have tried one last time for Bri,' Sue said with a sigh. Then looking up at Jane, she laughed softly. 'I suppose you think I'm daft.'

Jane shook her head slowly. 'No, nothing of the sort. I know you love Brian very much and a son is important to him.'

As Jane continued to examine Sue, she knew that she was the last one to condemn Sue for making a decision that seemed somewhat irrational. Her own behaviour wasn't so very different—an affair with a man who had once broken her heart. She had been through the pain once and would, no doubt, suffer again when he left—no, that wasn't logical thinking.

'See you next month?' Sue asked before she left. 'The antenatal clinic as usual?'

Jane nodded, smiling ruefully. 'As usual.'

When Sue had gone, Jane sat quietly, reflecting on the months that had passed since Marcus's and Ben's arrival. Everything about her life had changed. In the past she'd believed that she'd moved on from the days when it had only been Marcus and a family of their own that she had yearned for. She'd convinced herself that she was fulfilled with her career, her friends and social life in Nair.

But now she knew that to be false—in truth, there was nothing more she wanted than to settle down with the right man and have children. And there was only one man in her life—and always had been.

Almost two weeks later, on a sunny Saturday morning, Ben and Marcus stood on her doorstep, dressed in shorts and T-shirts. 'These are for you,' Ben announced as he reached up to hug her. After solemnly presenting her with a large packet of Cornwall toffee, he chased through to the lounge.

Marcus's gaze was wry. 'He couldn't wait to get here. Sara, Greg and the two boys delivered him home about an hour ago—the journey along the coastal road took them longer than they planned, so they had to dash off. Their flight out of Heathrow is booked for tomorrow.'

'Where's Donovan?' Ben called from the lounge.

'Why don't you go and see for yourself?' Jane went through and opened the French window.

While Ben was playing with Donovan by the pond, Marcus came up behind her and wrapped his arms around her waist. 'He missed you...'

'I didn't realise how much I'd missed him...' Jane sighed.

'I think it can safely be said that all the time he spent with his cousins hasn't quite matched the mysterious attraction of that cat,' Marcus whispered in her ear, pausing to nibble her ear lobe.

'Donovan knows when he's onto a good thing. Just look at the two of them.'

They watched, laughing at the cat and Ben as they played, chasing a tail of string across the rockery.

'Can I persuade you into a day spent in the company of two very attentive males?' Marcus murmured, tightening his grip around her waist.

She turned in his arms and threaded her arms around his neck. Looking up into his face, she pouted. 'That depends.'

'On what?'

'On how much encouragement I get...'

'Oh, I see. Like this?' He kissed her fully on the mouth. 'Was that enough?'

'Almost...'

He kissed her again and she laughed, gently pushing him away. 'So what would you like me to pack for the picnic?'

'Absolutely nothing. Today I'm taking you both to lunch.'

She raised her eyebrows in mock surprise.

'I've booked lunch for two o'clock at the Spyglass—a little hotel not far from here. Bring your swimsuit, too.'

She gave him a rueful smile. 'So you had everything planned?'

'Of course.' He laughed as Ben came running in.

'I wish we could stay here all day,' Ben said as Donovan followed.

A comment that caused Marcus to mumble a remark that no one heard.

The cosy hotel that Marcus had selected to eat at was every bit as enchanting as he'd described. With sea views across the Solent to the Isle of Wight, the dining room was decorated in modern colours and the walls festooned with bright sea prints. A soft breeze blew in through the open windows of the balcony, and after a light salad lunch they sat for a while in steamer chairs, taking in the view.

It was a perfect afternoon. They swam in the hotel pool and later had tea, before leaving for the beach. Strolling along the wet sand, they collected shells which were once again designated for Mrs Barnes's garden.

When Marcus and Jane collapsed on the sand, Ben remained at the water's edge by a rock pool, digging for crabs. Marcus sighed, leaning back on the blanket they'd brought with them. 'I suppose he's not going to want to go home tonight,' he murmured as he threw a teasing glance her way, adding, 'And neither will I.'

'Then stay.'

'At the cottage?'

'Why not? Ben can sleep in the spare room. And…there's the futon downstairs…'

Marcus grinned. 'Now, sleeping downstairs seems like rather a temptation…'

She laughed. 'One you'll have to resist.'

Marcus groaned, trailing a finger along her arm. 'It's still an offer I can't refuse.'

She giggled and, jumping to her feet, held out her hand. 'Come on. We've time for a last paddle.'

Marcus gripped her hand and muttered, 'No rest for the wicked.'

To which she remarked as they walked across the sand to join Ben, 'But tonight you'll have to be very, very good.'

CHAPTER ELEVEN

AT SIX o'clock on Monday morning Jane was up, trying to gargle away the hint of a vicious throat. After breakfast she went for a jog to the harbour to clear her head. It was a fine, warm morning and there was very little swell to the water. The horizon was dotted with fishing vessels and she stopped to admire the scene as she leaned over the harbour wall, but she felt too dizzy to pause for long.

Suddenly it was all she could do to drag herself back to the cottage and change for work.

'You look dreadful, Dr Court,' Paula said as Jane arrived at the surgery. 'Are you OK?'

'I'll be all right,' Jane said as she took a pile of patient records from Paula's hands.

'You're supposed to come back from a weekend refreshed.' Paula frowned. 'Is there anything I can do?'

'No, thanks, Paula.' Jane made a brave effort to smile, but she felt ghastly. She knew she had a temperature and her throat was burning. 'Who's on duty today?'

'Dr Jardine and you. And Dr Granger's on call.'

'I'd better make a start.' Jane hoped Paula hadn't noticed the sweat breaking on her top lip. 'Who's first?'

'A lady with her little boy—sore throat and temperature. Sounds like a virus. We seem to have an outbreak this morning.'

Jane nodded, turning to make her way along the corridor. Just as she arrived at her room her legs gave way and she almost fell in. A few seconds later she was leaning against Marcus who seemed to have sprung from nowhere.

'Good grief, you're burning up,' he muttered, sitting her down in the chair. 'How long have you been like this?'

'I felt a bit odd in the night.' Jane pushed her clammy hands over her face.

'Why in heaven's name didn't you stay in bed, girl?'

'Because I've got—'

'A viral infection,' growled Marcus as he took her temperature and felt the glands around her neck. His fingers were firm and skilful, and when he told her to open her mouth she could tell by his expression that there was no way she was going to stay at work. 'All the classic symptoms—raised temperature, an evil-looking throat and swollen glands. Home you go.'

'But my list, Marcus—' she protested as he hauled her up.

'Paula can give me your early patients. I've an hour before I go on my calls, and when I come back I can see those who are still here.'

'Oh, Marcus, I—'

'There's no way you're staying,' he told her with a gentle grin. 'We've enough casualties waiting out there, without adding to the queue. I suppose you've heard there's been an outbreak of flu?'

Jane nodded bleakly. 'You'll all be rushed off your feet.'

'I doubt it. Anyway, we'll cope. You're not indispensable.' As Marcus propelled her from surgery, telling the girls at Reception what was happening, Jane meekly submitted, feeling like a wrung-out dishrag.

When he got her home he undressed her, put her to bed and brought her up a jug of ice cold water. 'You stay put,' he warned her as he sat on the edge of the bed. She was shivering like a leaf. 'I'll be back to check on you this afternoon. If you need me, I'm on call. Pick up the phone and I'll be here in minutes.'

'You've done too much already,' she mumbled miserably.

'I know what I'd like to do,' he whispered gruffly. 'But you're at a disadvantage—and anyway there isn't time.'

She gave him a wobbly grin. 'Take my key, there on the dressing-table. You can let yourself in.'

He smiled, raising his eyebrows. 'Carte blanche, eh?' He tucked the sheet around her. 'Now...sleep, drink plenty of fluids, and I'll see you later.'

She was drifting off as she watched his tall figure move out of the door, and by the time the front door clicked she was fighting to stay awake.

Her rest was punctuated with hot sweats and frozen chills, but after a long while she did manage to sleep. And when Marcus came back later that day, she neither heard nor saw him. It was only in the night she sensed him there, stroking back her damp hair.

'Dad says he's bringing up the soup in a minute.' Ben's small voice caused her to open her eyes wider, stretch slightly and groan at her aching muscles.

She eased herself up on the pillow and stared foggily at the small figure standing beside the bed.

'Are you feeling better now?' Ben lowered the round bowl to the bedside table.

'Much, thank you, Ben.' She felt as weak as a kitten but the shivering had stopped. 'Is the water for me?'

Ben nodded at the bowl and flannel draped over the side. 'Dad said you might like it to freshen up with. I've just got to get the soap. I didn't put it in the water 'cos it would melt.'

'That's very thoughtful of you. Do you think you could find me a towel, too?'

Ben scampered off, the sound of his busy footsteps in the bathroom audible on the tiles. When he returned he carried the soap dish in one hand and a towel in the other.

Giving her a broad grin, he watched her as she rinsed the flannel and bathed her face. As she was burying her face in the towel, Donovan jumped up on the bed, his loud purr announcing his need for attention.

'I've fed him every day,' Ben said brightly, perching himself on the side of the bed. 'And taken him for walks.'

'Every day?' Jane repeated as she lowered the towel.

Ben nodded. 'We've been looking after you for two days 'cos you've been ill.' He grinned widely. 'Dad said you wouldn't mind us staying here, not if I kept my bedroom tidy and I looked after Donovan.'

At this, Marcus walked in, carrying a tray, and threw a rueful glance at Jane. 'Ah, how is our patient today?'

Jane managed a shaky grin. 'Thanks to your able assistant, feeling very much cleaner now.'

'And soon to be fed!' Marcus placed the tray on her lap. 'Welcome back to civilisation.'

She looked at them and through rather tearful eyes murmured, 'I don't know what to say.'

Marcus cast an arm around his son's shoulders and grinned. 'Don't say anything. Just be the perfect patient and finish your soup.'

The flu lasted another twenty-four hours but it wasn't until Friday that Jane felt able to walk safely around the house. She boasted to Marcus that she'd beaten it, but she felt shaky nevertheless.

'The only nice part is having your undivided attention,' Jane admitted ruefully at Friday lunchtime as they sat at the breakfast bar.

'Any time.' Marcus grinned. 'It comes with the service.' He gazed at her for a long while until finally he glanced at his watch. 'I must go. Darren's mother is bringing Ben back soon—don't make supper. I'll bring something home with me tonight.'

'I'm looking forward to seeing him. Perhaps we can walk down to the harbour.' The sun was streaming in the French windows and the garden was a hive of activity. She longed to be out in the fresh air.

'Don't attempt anything adventurous,' Marcus warned, reading her thoughts. 'Rest and enjoy.'

He washed their dishes, then came back to where she was sitting. Hunkering down beside her, he took her hand. His grey eyes were full of concern as he looked up at her. She reached out to run her hands through the shock of black hair that always looked so thick and glossy.

'Thank you both for looking after me,' she whispered, her voice catching.

'You can do the same for us,' he teased, 'if we fail to repel the miserable bug.'

Without making a response, she let herself take in the moment—a special moment, one that she knew she would remember long after they were gone from her life. His beautiful grey eyes against the faint blue of his summer shirt, his broad shoulders, the way the material strained across them as he moved. His sexy smile, his long, straight nose above full, generous lips.

'You'll both stay tonight?'

Lifting her hand to his lips, he nodded. 'We've no intention of leaving until our patient is fully recovered—though I have to admit the futon is protesting at the imposition of my weight.'

After he had gone she wandered into the garden and sat on the swing seat. Donovan jumped onto her lap and curled there contentedly. Whether it was the fact that Marcus and Ben would be there later, or relief that she was emerging from the half-world she had been in, she did as Marcus advised, and gave way to sleep.

*   *   *

The following Monday morning, another wave of viral casualties crowded the surgery and, feeling back to her old self, Jane fought her way through a hectic day. Her on-call duty meant she had broken sleep for the next two nights. Sore throats and high temperatures were the main offenders and there was little she could do to help her patients other than offer the same advice Marcus had given her.

Annie rang through with an emergency call at five. 'Brian Porcher on the phone, Dr Court,' she said hurriedly. 'And it doesn't sound too good.'

Ten minutes later, Jane was parking outside the small end-of-terrace house near the harbour and Brian was rushing towards her.

'I think something's happened to the baby,' he gasped, his face grey. 'Sue says she thinks she's having a miscarriage.'

As soon as Jane saw his wife lying on the sofa in their front room, her face contorted with pain, Jane feared the worst. After examining her, Jane called for an ambulance and half an hour later Sue was admitted to hospital.

Brian blew his nose on an oily handkerchief as he stood beside his wife. Lying on the gurney, Sue looked lifeless, only her dark brown hair relieving the ghostly white of her complexion.

'Don't take it so hard, Bri,' she whispered. 'It wasn't meant to be.'

The big man nodded and grasped his wife's hand, his ravaged face revealing the shock and disappointment of the last few hours. The complications associated with the incomplete miscarriage Sue had suffered meant that it would only be a few minutes before she was taken to Theatre.

'It's time we left,' Jane said quietly as the nursing team entered. She smiled briefly at Sue, then accompanied Brian to the waiting room.

'I just can't believe she lost so much blood,' Brian mut-

tered as she walked beside him. 'Will she be all right, Dr
Court?'

'Sue has every chance of recovery, Brian.' Jane wished
she could reassure him with more confidence, but Sue was
at a very low point. 'Now, don't you think you should go
home to the children? Who's looking after them?'

'My mother. I'll ring her.' Brian groaned, thrusting a
hand through his hair. 'I'm not leaving here.'

'You know that Sue will be in Theatre for some while?'

'I'm not leaving her, Dr Court,' Brian said again. 'Mum
will cope. I…I just feel so guilty. Going on about this baby
and ignoring the danger signs—how could I have been so
selfish?' The big man looked devastated and Jane felt sorry
for him.

'Is there anything I can do?' she asked.

He shook his head, struggling to speak as he lowered his
head. 'You don't know what you've got till you nearly lose
it, that's for sure. I love Sue. I don't want to lose her. But
I know you were right when you said we should have listened to the consultants. I just had this obsession about a
son and I couldn't get it out of my mind. I wish to God it
was me going down to Theatre, not her.'

Jane waited as he tried to recover himself then, when he
was composed, she accompanied him to the café. She left
him there to drink a reviving coffee, then made her way
out of the hospital. The big fisherman's words rang in her
mind as she drove back to the surgery, the irony of her own
situation not lost on her. To lose someone special in your
life was a salutary lesson in love, but one she hadn't reck-
oned on learning again.

Over the next few weeks Sue Porcher recovered from her
miscarriage and underwent her hysterectomy. Brian took
time away from his boat and helped cope with the kids.
Nancy Farlow's rodent ulcers abated and, despite her scep-

ticism, the cryosurgery began to take effect. But at the beginning of September the sad news came in of Mr Macauley's death.

'It was last night, at eleven,' Paula told her at Reception. 'Bronchopneumonia, I'm afraid. Poor old soul.'

Jane phoned the unit later in the morning. There was little to add to the information, but she was told that Timothy Lister had been present at the end. The funeral had been arranged by the authorities for the following week and Jane said she would attend.

It wasn't until later in the day, when she was in the office, that she saw Marcus's car pull up outside. Ben scrambled out and Marcus followed him, his tall figure moving swiftly across the car park.

Surgery was over and the reception girls were tidying up. There was laughter and joking as Marcus and Ben stopped to talk. Jane listened to their voices before attempting to meet them in the passageway.

Ben ran full pelt into her arms and hugged her, chattering so rapidly she could only listen and hug him tightly. Above Ben's head, Marcus's eyes met hers. They were the wonderful silvery grey that made her tremble, and in their expression she saw the same yearning, the same desperate need that was evident in her own.

And when he explained that Ben was staying with Darren for the night, Jane felt a guilty rush of pleasure at the thought of a night spent entirely on their own.

A thousand different scents pervaded the air as Jane lay awake in Marcus's arms, her body trembling with pleasure.

'Happy?' Marcus whispered as he drew her closer, sensing she was awake.

'Very.'

The silence deepened around them as Jane looked up into the shadowed features she knew so well. Marcus kissed her and she clung to him, loving the chafe of his chest hair against her naked breasts, the familiar rhythm of his body as his arousal seemed more passionate than ever.

It was as if their pent-up desires had finally been released, and with her eyes closed she buried his head against her breasts. Cradling him close, he moaned softly, gently biting each nipple, his tongue caressing their erect peaks. A shudder of need went through them both and she cried out, lost in the pleasure of her shattered senses.

After an age, he sank down beside her. Trembling with breathless fulfilment, she knew something had changed. It was as if in some way their unspoken doubts had been set aside and love flowed freely. Soothed by his contented breathing, she felt a brief pang of guilt at her refusal to consider the future as she fell asleep in his arms.

'Apart from wanting to take you straight back to bed this morning, I could eat seven men's breakfasts,' Marcus told her the following morning. 'I'm not quite sure which to do first before we collect the boys.'

Jane linked her arms around his neck, her blonde hair falling gently from her face. Her blue eyes were a soft, misty blue from their night of love, her lips bruised and tender with his kisses. She felt aroused again as his hands ran over her back.

'Flip a coin,' she whispered, unable to resist.

'I don't need to. I've made my decision,' he muttered as he swept her into his arms. 'Breakfast can wait.'

Unashamedly they spent the next hour in bed until, showered and changed into beach wear, they prepared to collect Ben and Darren. The boys were waiting in Darren's garden, beach balls and lilos piled at the gate. Marcus thanked Darren's mother while Jane ushered the boys into the car.

They ate a meal by the sea at a small café, Marcus and

the boys spoiling themselves with cooked breakfasts. Jane had little appetite, feeling shades of the nausea that had been present with the flu. She was content to sit under the umbrella on the beach, while Marcus and the boys explored the coves.

Darren was delivered home before it was dark, and once again Ben and Marcus stayed at the cottage. Despite a cloudy sky on Sunday, they had exhausted themselves by sunset, adventuring along the cliff paths. But alone at the cottage that night, Jane tried to ignore the nausea that returned. She went to bed early, deciding that sleep was the answer. In the morning, however, she felt even more queasy.

Frederick Macauley's memorial service was held at the crematorium chapel in Nair on a cloudless September morning. Jane hadn't expected Marcus to be there, but he arrived shortly after ten, sitting beside her as a few words were said by an official over the coffin.

Mr Macauley, a bachelor all his life, hadn't been a religious man. Little was known of him other than his sight had begun to fail him in midlife. Pensioned off from his job with a local transport firm, he'd had few neighbours who'd called on him and even fewer friends. At the rear of the small chapel Jane watched the mourners pay their last respects—several older men, a representative from the hospital unit and one young man dressed in a leather jacket.

'That's Timothy Lister,' Jane whispered. 'The crash victim you helped on your first day here. As I've told you, he was practically the only visitor Mr Macauley ever had, and was with him when he died.'

Marcus frowned and then, raising his eyebrows, glanced at Jane. 'A weird twist of fate, isn't it? Sometimes you wonder…'

But Marcus's voice tailed off as the short service ended

and they made their way out into the glorious September morning.

'Dr Granger?' Timothy held out his hand as he approached.

'Hello, there.' Marcus shook hands with the young man and smiled.

'I've never thanked you personally for what you did for me, but my life has changed in more than one respect since the accident.'

Jane glanced at Marcus, who remained silent, his brow creased with a slight frown.

'You see, not only did I have a second chance at life, but I lost a big chip I had on my shoulder. Both my parents died in a car accident when I was twelve. I got fostered out and never really settled. I suppose the speed thing I had was just a way of pushing my luck. But I realised in hospital that there were a lot of people less fortunate than I was. Including Fred.'

Marcus nodded slowly. 'Dr Court told me that you visited him.'

'Yeah, we kind of hit it off. You see, Fred never knew his parents and was brought up in a boys' home, so we had something in common. He joined the army and was a prisoner of war for three years. The things he went through were enough to turn anyone's hair grey. But he never told anyone, he said. Not till the end.'

Marcus nodded slowly. 'And you were with him…'

Timothy smiled. 'Yeah. And that's something I won't forget. I couldn't do it for my own parents, but being with Fred in his last hours kind of made up for them. As I say, all this has changed my life—and it's down to you that I survived.'

'I'm pleased it turned out well,' Marcus said quietly. 'Are you on the road again?'

'No way. Lost my licence after the accident. But I'm in

no hurry to drive again. I've got a bike now. That's fast enough for me for the time being.'

'Thank you for visiting Mr Macauley,' Jane said as the young man went to move away. 'I know it meant a great deal to him.'

Timothy shook his head. 'No, it meant a lot more to me, Dr Court.'

They watched the slim figure mount the bicycle propped against the chapel wall and cycle off. Jane looked up at Marcus. He smiled down at her and without words took her hand, squeezing it tightly.

They walked slowly to where the cars were parked and in the beauty of the September morning, paused to listen to the birds in the trees, their songs the only sounds to break the silence.

'The old chap found a kindred soul in the end,' Marcus said eventually. 'At least something positive came out of it all.'

Jane sighed, her thoughts too complex to analyse. 'It's amazing how things happen.'

'Like us,' Marcus said unexpectedly, his voice strained.

'You mean...' She searched his face, trying to guess what he meant. 'Meeting again?'

'No...no, not really,' he murmured distractedly. 'I was thinking of...Katrina...and how—'

But before he could say any more the mobile phone in his jacket began to ring and, closing his eyes briefly, he sighed, tugging it impatiently from his pocket. While he was speaking, Jane unlocked her car, parked next to Marcus's.

Vaguely she registered Marcus saying that he would be at a patient's house within a few minutes as an overwhelming urge to retch flowed over her. She sat in her car and slotted the key into the ignition. Her fingers were trembling as she tried to suppress the nausea.

'Must fly,' Marcus whispered as he bent down to kiss her. 'See you back at surgery this afternoon?'

She nodded, tasting the salt from his kiss on her lips, her voice over-bright as she answered, 'Yes...yes, of course.'

She watched him drive away, gazing through the open window. All the birds were singing, the sky was a cloudless, azure blue. The scent of autumn drifted through the dying leaves...as the nagging suspicion in her mind turned slowly to stomach-sinking certainty.

CHAPTER TWELVE

JANE had been sitting in the office, trying to concentrate on the post and wondering if she should have tried harder to eat breakfast. But ignoring the nausea she had woken up with was impossible. Food had had no appeal lately. Especially breakfast. And she knew why. She had made the test and it showed a positive result. She had to face the truth.

She was pregnant.

As she was trying to quell the waves of sickness, Phil entered, waving a letter in his hand. 'October,' he told her breathlessly. 'We've got a completion date for October.' He raised his eyebrows, laying the letter on the desk before her. 'We'll have to start advertising for a fourth member. Do you think Marcus will wait until we find someone?'

She nodded slowly. 'Yes, I'm sure he will.'

'He tells me that he and Ben have decided to go for that holiday with his sister—Florida isn't it?'

Jane nodded. For the last week even Ben had been talking about the promised holiday with his aunt and uncle and the visit to Disneyland. It was a topic that had even taken precedence over his new term at school. Marcus had said very little.

She knew it was what they had agreed on all those months ago and what, at the time, they had both wanted. As time had gone by she'd tried to fight her feelings for him, then, knowing the struggle had been useless, she'd made the decision to enjoy their relationship while she could. She knew that it had to come to an end—Marcus had never given her reason to think otherwise.

Somehow they had avoided confronting the issue, perhaps because neither of them wanted to regret their last days together. She wanted them to remember the days as happy. But now she was pregnant.

The word whirled around in her mind. When could it have happened? She had been careful to take the Pill, yet there had been the flu. And she had felt so ill then...had been totally out of it for two days when Ben and Marcus had looked after her. Now she had missed her period—and the test had confirmed her suspicions. But tests were occasionally wrong, she argued with herself. Then she was engulfed by a wave of nausea and knew that nothing but the pregnancy could explain that.

'Should take us about a week to transfer,' Phil was saying as he sat down beside her at the desk. 'I've a private firm coming in to help with the technology and a removals company lined up for the furniture and equipment. Jean and I are working out free time for the staff so everyone can settle in. With a bit of luck doors should open the second week in October.' Phil glanced at her, his brow creased in a deep frown. 'Well, this is it, goodbye to the old surgery.' He looked around the room with its overflowing carousel and shelves stacked full of papers and files. 'I'll miss it, you know.'

Jane nodded. 'Yes, me, too, Phil.'

'It will be a new beginning, changes for the better. And with all the new hi-tech stuff, we won't know ourselves.'

They both lapsed into silence and Jane was aware that they had both become lost in their thoughts. She knew that a separation from the old family surgery was a big transition, and Phil must have memories of Maggie linked to this place.

Jane looked around the white stone walls bearing little scraps of paper stuck to the corkboards, the inspirational notes and the wry jokes. There were memories for her here

as well. Nair Surgery had been her rock. It was here she
had learnt to live without Marcus.

Now all that had changed. Marcus had come here and
all her defences had crumbled. She'd allowed herself to fall
in love again and a child had been conceived. She was
carrying his baby and he was leaving. What was she to do?
a voice of panic wailed inside her. What could she do?
What choices did she have?

For the rest of the week there was an air of excitement
about the place. Even the patients seemed to welcome the
news. The girls on Reception began the unenviable job of
sorting, sifting and packing things into cardboard boxes.
And Jane began to make her own list of priorities, though
her mind for most of the time revolved around her pregnancy. She would take another test... But for some reason
she kept putting it off, refusing to accept the truth.

'Can I help?' Marcus said the following Friday evening
as he walked into Jane's room and found her on her knees.
She was stacking all the rubbish she could find into a bin
liner. Her surgery was long over, but she needed to make
a start. She looked up, pushing back her hair, to find
Marcus frowning down.

'I don't know what to keep and what to trash,' she complained exhaustedly. 'It's so hard to get rid of old corre-
spondence. It's not important, but it's still hard to throw
away.'

He sat on the chair beside her, his fingers reaching out
to knead the muscles around her neck. 'Let me take you
away from all this,' he whispered, amusement and sympathy in his voice. 'How about breakfast tomorrow morning?'

She looked up at him then. 'Yes...I'd like that.'

'You look...oh, just...very lovely.' His gaze met her

distracted blue eyes. 'Stay still. I'm taking a mental picture—a photograph in my mind to file away...'

She looked down and bit her lip hard, a sob choked back in her throat. She pushed it down firmly—he would think she was mad if she burst into tears right now. But she felt like it—oh, how she yearned to lay her head against his chest and beg him to stay. And tell him life meant nothing unless he was with her. And, of course, to tell him about the baby...

Instead, she forced a bright, wobbly smile on her lips. 'Will Ben be coming with us?' He stared at her, still frowning, but she looked away, thrusting rubbish into the bag.

'No, Ben's out tomorrow with Darren and his parents.' He paused, watching her movements, then, when she wouldn't look up at him, he asked cautiously, 'Could I invite myself back to the cottage after breakfast?'

She nodded, not daring to stop what she was doing.

'Jane?'

She practised a smile at the bin liner and finally looked up. 'But it will cost you some ground coffee. I'm out of the fresh—'

'Listen to me,' he interrupted gruffly, catching hold of her chin and turning it towards him. 'Stop what you're doing and come here.'

'But someone might come in.' She resisted his attempt to draw her against him.

'Jane...don't shut me out,' he pleaded.

She knew she was doing just that. She knew her defences were going up to stop the pain. But she closed her eyes and choked back the despair as he pulled her into his arms and kissed her. And it was then, at that moment, she knew that she could never destroy what was growing inside her. Not that a termination had ever been a consideration, even though, had one of her patients come to her in such a situation, the choice would have been a strong possibility.

As she opened her eyes and gazed into Marcus's face, the other option—of telling him—was so strong she almost blurted it out. Then the voice inside her warned her that this wasn't the moment. Tomorrow she would tell him. Tomorrow when they had time together and she had composed herself.

Tomorrow.

All night she tossed and turned, considering the repercussions of such a disclosure. There was no way she wanted him to feel trapped, or to stay with her because of the baby. He had never sought her out after Katrina had died and she could only assume his love hadn't been as enduring as hers—or he would have. Perhaps his feeling for Katrina had overshadowed the love they'd once shared, or perhaps the time that had elapsed had proven too great a test—and love had simply melted away.

She had no answers to the past, but the future was in her hands, she reminded herself as she cast her mind back to that initial interview. Marcus had been firm in his resolve to leave Nair when the new surgery was complete.

By morning, Jane was convinced that telling Marcus she was pregnant could only bring resentment and distrust into their relationship. And knowing Marcus's feelings about children, he would want to do the right thing. She shuddered at the very thought of those words. How could a relationship be built on anything but love? And he had never said that word...never uttered it...

And what of Ben? How could he be expected to understand? Far better he should leave Nair remembering the kind of friendship that they'd forged. Then, at least, there would be no recriminations and no regrets.

Marcus took her to a small café by the harbour, but she didn't get more than a slice of toast down before the waves of nausea returned.

'What's wrong?' Marcus asked her, diving into eggs and bacon.

'Nothing. It's just a little early. Maybe I'll have something later.'

'You haven't eaten properly since the bug.' Marcus commented.

'Maybe it's still lingering.' She shrugged.

They walked back to the cottage under the umbrella. September rain seemed to have set in and they lay in bed, listening to the drops falling from the gutters onto the windowsill. Marcus's warm body wrapped around her, fitting perfectly as he always did. Their love-making was blissful. Here in bed, for a short while, she forgot he was leaving, forgot the baby—and everything except the release of her emotions.

It was afternoon by the time they surfaced and showered. Dressed in jeans and sweaters, they mooched around the kitchen and made coffee. Marcus seemed quiet and it wasn't until they sat drinking it in the lounge on the sofa that he turned to her and said, 'Phil has found a GP. A married guy with a small daughter. His wife's a staff nurse at Southampton.' He paused. 'He's lined up the interview for Tuesday.'

The shock of what he had just told her caused her to catch her breath. A band of iron seemed to tighten around her ribs.

'It's what he hoped for,' Marcus continued in a flat voice. 'You'll move in to the new place with a full team. No glitches by the looks of it.'

Jane felt as though she were in a dream. It had finally come. The news she had been fearing. The end.

'And you?'

'Me?' She turned slowly, her anxious eyes going up to meet his.

'How do you feel…about the move…about everything?' he prompted.

'I feel…' She shrugged, tearing her eyes away lest they reveal the truth. 'I feel…oh, I don't know…' After a minute, she croaked, 'I—I'll miss you, Marcus. I'll miss you both.'

He turned and, removing the mug from her hands and lowering to the table, he pulled her into his arms, kissing her and murmuring softly, but his voice was so ragged that she couldn't hear his words.

Jane confirmed the pregnancy a week later. She went on as if in the same dream, a twilight world, occasionally coming out of it to make plans for the future, almost as though on autopilot. Trying to picture herself and the baby and telling herself that at least she would have the child to remember him by.

It was a fortnight before Marcus was due to leave that she overheard Paula talking to Annie at Reception.

'With my youngest, I was sick right up until my fifth month,' Paula was saying, unaware of being overheard. 'But other than that, pregnancy was a breeze.'

As Annie commiserated, Jane walked into her room, closed the door behind her and placed her hands slowly over her stomach. It was really happening to her. She was carrying Marcus's baby—their child. Suddenly a wild joy filled her, a euphoria that made her dizzy with pleasure. Then came reality—and the threads of sensible reasoning she had been trying to follow since the discovery of her pregnancy.

Bringing up a child on her own. Without a father. Could she do it? Her responsibilities at the new practice—with Phil relying on her to fulfil them. How would she cope with work and the baby? Crazy thoughts whirled around in her mind. But many women coped, she assured herself. Professional women like herself with a full working agenda and yet just as capable and loving as a parent.

A single parent.

A single working parent. There would be maternity leave to arrange and three months breastfeeding the baby. Then she would have to find help once she returned to work. She would be supporting the child—she would have its future in her hands. And for one terrifying moment she was filled with uncertainty.

Then slowly she composed herself and the fear subsided. By the time surgery was over she was calm again. She loved Marcus, had always loved him, but she wouldn't use her pregnancy to keep him. He would stay and do his duty—as he had done by Katrina. He was that kind of man. And she didn't want him on those terms. The only reason she would accept for Marcus staying would be that he loved her—unconditionally.

And that, as she well knew, hadn't happened.

It was a crisp, dry September Sunday and Cenna had decided to accept Jane's offer of lunch to celebrate the completion date for the new surgery. Next month they would all be transferred and the old surgery would open its doors for the last time.

For the occasion Cenna chose to wear a pale grey suit, teaming it with a soft white silk blouse and white high-heeled slingbacks. She wondered if she had dressed too formally for a Sunday lunch. But, then, Phil would be wearing something decent since he was on call, and she knew Jane would look gorgeous.

As Cenna arrived at Jane's cottage she wasn't surprised to see Marcus's BMW and Phil's Mercedes parked outside. The door opened and she was welcomed by Ben, dressed in jeans and a dark blue shirt, his hair combed neatly over his head.

'Hello, Dr Lloyd,' Ben said in a rather subdued manner.

'Hi, Ben. Am I late?'

'No, everyone's here. But we haven't started lunch yet.'

Jane appeared then, removing an apron to reveal a pale green silk dress that clung to her slim figure. Her blonde hair was drawn up in a chignon and her cheeks were flushed. She bent forward and they hugged.

'You look lovely,' Jane said as Ben disappeared. 'We're just about ready to eat.'

Cenna stepped into the hallway, a delicious aroma of roast beef and potatoes filling the air. 'Smells gorgeous, Jane. This is really wonderful—I can't remember when I last ate a roast lunch. Last Christmas, I think.'

Jane smiled as she beckoned Cenna to follow her. 'I thought it would be nice for us all to have one last get-together before the move.'

'I can't believe we actually have a date and a possible new partner,' Cenna admitted as she followed Jane into the kitchen. 'I hope he likes us.'

'Phil seems to be impressed. The interview went well, I understand. He's coming again to meet us. I did consider asking him today, but I thought it might seem a little too pressurised.'

'Yes, possibly.' Cenna sighed as she leaned against the worktop. 'It's hard to imagine Marcus not part of the team. I really will miss him. Has he set a date for leaving?'

'Yes, I believe so.' Jane glanced at her quickly. 'The day before John Hill starts.'

'Is there no chance of him changing his mind?'

'Phil asked me that and the answer, I'm afraid, seems to be no.' Jane turned away and busied herself with folding the napkins.

But Cenna had already seen the sadness in her friend's

eyes. 'Jane, you can't let him go, not if you love him. And you do, don't you?' For a moment she waited as Jane turned her back, her shoulders drooping under her dress.

'Cenna…if he had wanted to stay, he would have. But he has never said he wanted to—even when he joined us.'

'He may have been waiting for you to ask him stay. It could be as simple as telling him how you feel, Jane. Have you considered that?'

Jane paused before she answered. 'Would you ask the man you loved to abandon his plans for the future?'

The kitchen seemed very quiet and Cenna, at last, shook her head. 'Put like that,' she sighed softly, 'I suppose not. But it's such a waste—you two. You seem so right together. And surely you're entitled to a second chance after what happened with Katrina?'

'Perhaps the past would always come between us—' Jane began, then swayed against the table.

'Jane, what's wrong?' Cenna moved forward, but Jane looked white.

'S-sorry…' she mumbled, and fled.

Five minutes later Cenna was standing beside Jane in the bathroom, attempting to offer some words of support—none of which, she realised after what Jane had just told her, would help.

CHAPTER THIRTEEN

THERE was no easy way to say goodbye. And there was Ben to consider...

In the end they went to a movie in Southampton, one Ben had been wanting to see. They ate at a pizza restaurant afterwards. It was a Thursday and Jane's day off, so it didn't seem out of the ordinary to meet up and share what had become a familiar ritual after Ben came home from school.

The painful goodbyes lasted only a few minutes that night. Jane knew that Marcus wouldn't stay at the cottage. They were leaving on Saturday and Jane had accepted the final time they had made love—the weekend before—as their personal goodbye.

On Sunday morning she lay awake, listening to the bells peal over Nair, with Donovan curled on the end of the bed. She could hardly look at him without thinking of Ben. But, then, what didn't remind her of Ben and Marcus?

She missed them more than she could have thought possible the following week. And it was change-over week. Whilst Cenna and Phil remained at the old surgery, it had been allotted to Jane and John Hill, the new GP, to begin at the new premises.

But despite the change of environment and activity, Jane's mind constantly wandered to the house on the Westcliffe, to the large, airy rooms of Mrs Barnes's Hillcrest which would be empty now.

It was on the Wednesday, early in the morning, that she suddenly felt the loss most keenly. She had arrived early at the new site, parking her car in the brand-new car park.

The precinct of shops nearby was already busy, but instead of the silent and cool sea breeze that blew down the hill against the whitewashed walls of Nair Surgery, there were baking and petrol smells and the inevitable background sound of town traffic. And over it all a weak sun shone down on the red-tiled roof and smoky glass doors of the new premises.

Jane helped Paula unlock, inhaling the aroma of new carpeting and upholstery as they entered.

'Gorgeous, isn't it?' Paula remarked as they made their way to the office down the long, light corridor. 'I'm only just finding my way around, though. How do you like your new rooms, Dr Court?'

Glancing at the pale blue door to the rooms that had been allotted to her halfway along the hall, she smiled. 'I'm finding having a treatment area of my own quite strange,' she admitted, raising her eyebrows as she began to take off her coat. 'But I'm glad I brought my old desk and chair—they make it seem like home.'

Paula laughed softly. 'I know what you mean. I keep looking around for the old carousel. The new files are great—but they take a bit of getting used to. What—or rather whom I miss most though, is Dr Granger. I can't believe he's gone. He seemed like a part of the furniture and...' The receptionist shrugged, her words tailing off as the phone began to ring in the office. 'Oh, well, that's something that hasn't changed.' She laughed, quickly glancing at her watch. 'Half past seven on the dot! Better go.'

As Jane walked slowly towards her room, Paula's words echoed in her head. Paula had said she couldn't believe Marcus had gone. And that was the way she felt, too. No telephone call, nothing in the post, not even a card. No word at all. Not even from Ben, who had promised to send her a card from the airport.

Had they forgotten her already?

The thought was too depressing and, attempting to turn her attention to the day ahead, she entered the impressive new rooms, aware that part of her still refused to let go of the past.

Later that week Timothy Lister, now resident in Nair, signed on as a new patient at the surgery. Sue Porcher arrived for a post-operative check and Jane found her to be well and reasonably happy. Brian, she said, had gone into the haulage business with Clyde Oakman, leaving the sea for dry land.

'There's always doubt on the future of fishing,' she explained as she sat with her youngest daughter on her knee. 'So when the opportunity came Brian took it. And after the miscarriage, I think he needed to find a new challenge.'

Jane could understand the Porchers' change in direction, but she was surprised when Nancy Farlow arrived, presenting her with a small sculpture for her room.

'It was down to you I took the plunge jobwise,' she said as Jane unwrapped the delicate wings of a seagull on a plinth. 'I'm selling my work now from the souvenir shops—sale or return. The money isn't anywhere as good as in the City, but I shan't be going back. In a way, the skin cancer helped me. I've a fresh perspective on life. I asked myself what I was doing, running round in circles to catch my tail. And I couldn't come up with an answer. It was then I decided to make the change—and I don't regret it one bit.'

But despite the positive outcomes of her patients' problems, Jane felt curiously removed from it all. On Saturday she was on call, while Phil and Cenna spent one last day at the old surgery. Jane hadn't returned there, careful to remove all her possessions during the previous weeks. She didn't want to see Marcus's room again. She could cope, she told herself firmly, if she wasn't reminded.

But it was on Saturday evening, when her calls were completed, that she found herself driving past the old surgery. Cenna's car was there and, pulling in to the drive, she got out and walked across toward the familiar white walls, glowing in the dusk.

The gulls screeched above, reminding her of Nancy's sculpture, and with the sound came a rush of memories—the first day Marcus was here, seeing him again, watching him fight to save Timothy Lister's life. Then there was Ben running across from the school bus, and in her cramped old room Frederick Macauley lying in Marcus's arms. Suddenly her eyes filled with tears and she turned away, her courage failing her.

For a while she steadied herself against the cold wind, breathing in its comforting familiarity. Then shakily she made her way towards the slope that marked the perimeter of the car park.

Taking the footpath across the field, she came to the sign that warned of danger, and made her way along the uneven trail towards the cliff. At its farthest point, the path provided a breathtaking view over the bay. She wanted to see the blue waters of Nair harbour one last time…

She shivered as the icy wind penetrated her coat, but she finally arrived at the end of the path. Lifting her collar, she huddled into its warmth, staring out over the darkening bay. The wind whipped at her hair and stung her cheeks. She braced herself against it, blinking away the salt and tears that stung her eyes.

It was as she moved forward that the sandy earth beneath her feet gave way. Her last memory was of the sea crashing against the boulders below as she lost her balance and fell towards them.

* * *

Cenna clutched the phone tightly. She had given all the details she knew of—it was up to Heathrow now. Once again another uncertain voice on the end of the line spoke, asking her to repeat her request.

'Yes, it's Granger…Dr Marcus Granger. G-r-a-n-g-e-r. Florida…yes. He's travelling with his son, Ben. It's very important you pass the message to him before he boards. Can you do that? Yes, all right, you have my number. I'll wait for his call.'

Cenna glanced out of the office window and saw the consultant, Martin Freeman, talking to a staff nurse. She caught his eye, indicating the phone, and he nodded. Returning her gaze to the telephone, Cenna willed it to ring, although she knew that it would be an outside chance that they could find Marcus. It was a quarter to eleven. From what she recalled from the conversation she'd had with Marcus at Jane's cottage, the flight time was around eleven o'clock.

Why had she left it this late? she argued with herself. Why in heaven's name hadn't she acted last night? She had even recalled the name of the hotel. She could have rung— she *should* have rung.

'Did you find him?' Martin Freeman entered the office and, folding his reading spectacles into the pocket of his dark blue suit jacket, he frowned at Cenna.

'I think I'm probably too late.'

'Does he know about the baby?'

Cenna shook her head.

The consultant nodded slowly as a sympathetic smile crossed his lips. 'She's a very fortunate young woman. Very fortunate indeed. With plenty of bed rest and a positive outlook, I see no reason why both mother and baby shouldn't do well.'

Cenna watched the consultant leave, relieved that the consultant had asked very few questions. She had revealed nothing other than that the father of the child was about to leave the country that morning—a fact she had discovered in her last conversation with Marcus at Jane's house. He'd confided he was to spend another week in London in order to show Ben the City.

The minutes ticked slowly by and Cenna stared at the telephone, willing it to ring. But as the silence deepened she accepted that hope was fading. Once the plane was in the air, it would be too late.

Then, as the hands of her watch indicated eleven-fifteen, the telephone rang.

'Dr Lloyd speaking.' Cenna held her breath as she waited for the reply, aware of the staff sister's presence in the office.

'Cenna?'

'Oh, Marcus…thank goodness.' She turned slightly and raised her eyebrows, the older woman nodding before discreetly leaving the office.

'Cenna? What's happening? What's wrong?' Marcus spoke quickly, in his usual even tone, but Cenna recognised the concern in it and took a deep breath.

'Marcus—I'm at Southampton General. It's Jane. She had a fall last night—'

'A fall? Where?' Marcus broke in anxiously.

'It was near the old surgery. She'd gone along the path beyond the perimeter fence. Heaven knows why. The path is never used these days, it's too dangerous.'

'Oh, my God.' Marcus groaned. 'How did you know where she was?'

'I saw her car,' Cenna told him quickly. 'When I couldn't find her I guessed she must have walked down to the cliff. Luckily her fall was broken by a ridge about thirty feet below. She…she suffered concussion and has broken her clavicle. The rest is mainly bruising and—'

'Is she conscious now?' Marcus broke in again.

Cenna took a deep breath. 'Yes, she is.'

'I'll come straight away.'

'But your flight—'

'Never mind about that. I'll be with you as soon as I can. And, Cenna?'

'Yes?'

There was a pause before Marcus murmured huskily, 'Thanks.'

The distress in his voice was evident and Cenna knew she had done the right thing in contacting him, no matter what Jane's reasons were for not telling him about the baby.

'She'll be fine—when she sees you,' Cenna replied quietly, praying she was right.

'Darling…' The murmured word drifted into Jane's consciousness and floated softly around in her mind. 'Darling…' There it was again, a word so precious and yearned for she imagined she must be dreaming it. She hoped the dream would continue and erase the dull physical ache that seemed to envelop her body.

Jane slowly opened her eyes, their lids so heavy they felt lead-weighted. Her inclination was to close them again, but she made an effort, sensing a figure leaning over her, blocking out the light.

'Jane…Jane, darling, it's me, Marcus.'

A tender hand smoothed through her hair. A soft kiss melted on her forehead. Warm lips caressed her skin…skin that had felt so bruised and battered the last time she had woken. By some miracle his lips didn't disappear but remained there, resting softly on her cheek.

'Oh, my sweet, my love…what happened? Why didn't you tell me? Oh, God, Jane, the baby—*our* baby—why didn't you tell me?'

She tried to shake her head. 'I…I couldn't. You and Ben…you had so much planned…'

'We have nothing—absolutely nothing without you. We wanted to stay—but I needed to hear you wanted it, too.' He held her close, as close as the bandaging on her arm and shoulder would allow. 'Our baby is safe,' he muttered shakily, his voice breaking for a moment until with a firm effort he resumed his control. 'Do you hear me, darling? Our baby is going to survive. The life we created between us.'

'Yes…I hear you.' The tears escaped down her cheeks, slipping wetly into the neck of the hospital gown.

Marcus bent low, his face buried in her hair, his thumbs gently stroking the dampness from her skin. For a long while he remained there, his hands laying lightly on her body, so lightly that she knew he was afraid of hurting her. Finally, resting his palms on either side of her, he looked down, his grey eyes filled with concern.

'The ground…it…it just gave way,' she croaked. 'And then I was falling. And…and everything went black.'

'You hit your head as you fell,' Marcus explained softly. 'Cenna found you. She managed to climb down and stay with you until help came.'

Suddenly it all came flooding back—the wind in her face, the earth giving way and the rock striking her head. Then the excruciating pain in her shoulder and arm before she blacked out. 'Oh, Marcus, you're telling me the truth?' she begged as he held her as close as he could. 'The baby is…is all right?'

His lips moved against her cheek. 'You've had a scan…the baby's fine…but from here on in, abseiling is definitely out of the question.'

A mixture of laughter and tears welled up in the back of her throat as she looked up at him. 'I…I can't believe you're here.'

'You'd better believe it,' he muttered gruffly, his grey

eyes narrowing. 'Because I'm going to be around for a very long time to come.'

'You mean…' she faltered, 'you're going to be here—in Nair?'

'I mean, in your life, where I should have been years ago. And if Nair is where you're happiest, then that's all that matters.'

Helplessly she stared up at him, unable to believe what he was saying.

'I mean it, Jane.' His eyes held hers. 'You, the baby and Ben are my life. Wherever you are, I will be, too. If only you hadn't left London…'

It was then she knew she had to tell him. And as the words came out in a confused tumble she began to drift, his face dimming as she clung to his hand, wondering if, when she woke, he would still be there.

As Jane drew the blinds a gleaming white frost sparkled on the rooftops, despite the pale December sun. Marcus tooted his horn and she waved. Still wearing their dressing-gowns, Jane and Ben stood in the kitchen after breakfast, gazing out of the window partially obscured by a preening Donovan.

'How long will Dad be?' Ben asked eagerly as he climbed on the stool in time to wave at the disappearing BMW.

'Not long, darling. Saturday surgery finishes at twelve.'

'Are we going out this afternoon?'

Jane raised her eyebrows doubtfully. 'Well, although we don't leave for our flight until Monday, I think we should all start packing.' Her heart gave a little flutter as she thought of their Christmas holiday, now only two days away.

'I can't wait to go to Disneyland!' Ben exclaimed suddenly. 'I'm really excited.'

Jane snaked an arm around his small shoulders. 'Me, too. I'm only sorry that you had the disappointment of not going in October.'

He shrugged casually. 'I wasn't *really* disappointed, 'cos even though I wanted to go on holiday, I didn't really want to leave here.' He gave her a mischievous grin. 'And now everything's even better. We're all going together.'

Taking a deep breath, she nodded, hardly able to believe it herself. So much had happened in two months. Their low-key, heart-wrenchingly beautiful marriage service at the registry office, a Christmas honeymoon in Florida—and the most wonderful news of all, that the baby had suffered no ill effects from her accident. To add to this, Ben's delight at having a step-mum and a brother or sister as well had completed their happiness.

Sometimes she pinched herself to make sure she wasn't dreaming. And when that didn't work, instructing Marcus to pinch her was no help at all. Now that he was sleeping in her bed—legally—the pinching frequently turned into far more interesting pursuits.

'And after the holiday's over we're never, never going to move from Nair, are we?' Ben was prompting, his small brow puckered under a tousled mop of black hair.

'No, unless it's close by—to a larger house,' Jane assured him.

'I like it here.' This was said resolutely and Jane gazed down into her stepson's beautiful brown eyes. A wave of love crested in her chest, reaching almost epic proportions. 'I know you do, darling,' she told him gently. 'But when your baby brother or sister comes along, you won't want him waking you in the night. And babies, you know, can be very noisy. They need a room of their own.'

'He can sleep in mine,' Ben offered eagerly. 'I *want* him to be noisy. Like me.'

Jane laughed. 'It might not be a baby brother either. What if you have a sister?'

A shy grin tugged at his lips. 'Darren's got two sisters and they're really nice. Emma even tried to kiss me once.' His cheeks turned a bright pink. 'It was yuk!'

She gave in then to the urge to cuddle him, one in a long line of cuddles that she knew she was going to have to ration if, as Marcus frequently reminded her, Ben was to preserve even the slightest bit of street cred.

'Can I phone Darren and ask him to come over? I want to give him his Christmas present.'

'I don't see why not.'

He jumped down from the stool and, careful to avoid the large tabby cat at his feet, scampered into the hall. A few seconds later he returned, and Jane looked round in surprise.

'Have you phoned Darren already?'

Ben shook his head, moving slowly towards her. Surprised and overwhelmed, she gave herself up to the luxury of a voluntary hug, given with a love that only last year she could never have expected to receive.

After he had gone to phone Darren, Jane stayed where she was, treasuring a moment of delirious pleasure as she listened to his voice in the hall. Nothing could have made her or Marcus happier than to be reassured that Ben welcomed this baby, and she sighed ecstatically.

Life had its *very* special moments.

'Is he asleep?' Jane asked softly as Marcus came down the stairs, his long legs clad in jeans.

'Totally out of it.'

'He's been so excited…'

'That's an understatement. I think he must have packed his bag three times over.' Marcus grinned. 'I'm just surprised he didn't stow Darren in it, too.'

Jane giggled as he took her in his arms.

'Coffee in the lounge?' Marcus whispered, nuzzling her ear.

'I'll make it.' Jane turned toward the kitchen.

He grabbed her. 'No, you don't. Go and sit by the fire. Doctor's orders.'

She pouted. 'You both spoil me.'

'We have a vested interest.' Marcus drew his hand over the slight swell of her stomach. 'You have no conception of how much I'm looking forward to this child. Frankly, I've even had my doubts that I should allow you to fly. Your shoulder has only just begun to feel comfortable. And with a six-hour flight and then the journey to Sara's before you can really get a good night's sleep...'

She thought he was serious and was about to protest when the smile he gave her and the kiss he planted on her lips told her he was only teasing.

'Now, do as you're told.' He gave her a small push.

'Happy?' Marcus murmured a few minutes later as, coffee made, he drew her against him on the sofa.

Jane laid her head on his chest. 'I've never been so happy.'

The fire crackled cosily and Marcus took her hand, laying it with his on the slope of her stomach. 'Oh, Jane, I love you—both—so much.'

'Say it again, darling.'

'I love you, I love you, I love you...' He grinned as he tilted her chin, forcing her to look at him. 'Now it's your turn.'

'I've told you every day since the accident...'

'And I still haven't heard it enough.'

'Can I confess something first?' She didn't wait for his answer or she might never tell him. 'You know, I felt desperate when Sara arrived here in the summer. I didn't want to meet her. And I certainly couldn't cope with a holiday in Cornwall. And now we're going on our honeymoon and staying with her, and everything is—is *so* different. But I feel guilty—I was so afraid of losing you for the second time.'

'Oh, God, Jane…' He paused as if trying to find the right words. 'I wanted you to stop me from leaving Nair. I needed you to tell me you wanted me in your life. I didn't know what you felt. And every time I tried to discuss Katrina or the past you changed the subject.'

Jane sank against him. She couldn't look into his eyes. 'I was frightened. I didn't want to hear you say…say that you'd loved her…'

He was silent as the beating of her heart grew unbearably fast. Then gently he prised her away from him. 'Darling, I married Katrina because she needed me. For Ben's sake I tried to make her happy and feel secure. But I ached— yearned for you. For what we had lost. For the mistake I made in letting you go. I've never loved anyone in my life the way I love you.'

'Oh, Marcus.' She groped helplessly for the words.

'But there was nothing I could do. You left London and I had to accept your decision to end our relationship. I had no idea Katrina's attitude had changed. It was only in the hospital, when you told me, that I realised how selflessly you behaved.'

'I couldn't tell you before—it just seemed so unfair to Katrina.'

He nodded. 'I understand now—but at the time I was confused and angry. And after Katrina's death when I still didn't hear from…' He shrugged, looking deeply into her eyes. 'All I could do was to hope that you would return. But as the months turned into years I began to give up hope.' His eyes held hers in the flickering light of the fire. 'Eventually I came to a decision, which involved a lie— the only lie I have ever told you.'

She swallowed, suddenly afraid to hear. 'Go on.'

'It was the day I came for the interview. The truth is...I knew you were here in Nair. I'd discovered where you were from the surgery you worked with in London. I came to Nair for only one reason—and that was you.'

She stared up at him. 'You...you came to Nair because of me? Not because of Ben's asthma?'

He nodded, his eyes lowering. 'It was a bonus that Ben's asthma should get better...but if you'd been living on the other side of the world, I would have found you.' For a long while they gazed at one another, then Jane began to laugh, very softly at first, until they were hugging and laughing together and Marcus held her against him, his hand caressing the gentle curve of her stomach.

'Our baby,' he breathed elatedly. 'I can't believe it, Jane. I'm so happy.'

She clung to him, astonished she could love him so much. 'I've longed for this child, Marcus. All those years without you. Each day I wondered what it would have been like if we'd had our family.'

'I wondered, too. But when I found you, you were so changed, so assured, so self-contained. I didn't know if there was room in your life for us.'

'I love you, Marcus. I've always loved you.'

He took her hands and kissed each finger, then leaned across and kissed her mouth. 'I'm almost convinced,' he muttered, a smile on his lips as he lifted the wisps of silky blonde hair from her face to tuck them behind her ear.

'Then, I think,' she whispered, turning to link her arms around his neck, 'we should clear up any misunderstanding that still remains—before we go on honeymoon.'

'Absolutely,' he agreed softly, stretching out to turn off the lamp.

MILLS & BOON®

Makes any time special™

Mills & Boon publish 29 new titles every month. Select from...

Modern Romance™   Tender Romance™

Sensual Romance™

Medical Romance™   Historical Romance™

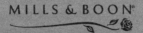

MILLS & BOON®

Medical Romance™

THE CONSULTANT'S CONFLICT *by Lucy Clark*

Book one of the McElroys trilogy

Orthopaedic surgeon Jed McElroy refused to see past
Dr Sally Bransford's privileged background and
acknowledge her merits. He fought his attraction to
her, but as they worked side by side, the prospect of
making her a McElroy was becoming irresistible!

THE PREGNANT DOCTOR *by Margaret Barker*

Highdale Practice

Dr Adam Young had supported GP Patricia Drayton at
the birth of her daughter, even though they'd just met!
Reunited six months later, attraction flares into passion.
Her independence is everything, but the offer of love
and a father for Emma seems tantalisingly close...

THE OUTBACK NURSE *by Carol Marinelli*

In isolated Kirrijong, Sister Olivia Morrell had her wish
of getting away from it all, and Dr Jake Clemson
suspected that she had come to the outback to get
over a broken heart. If she had to learn that not all men
were unreliable, could he be the one to teach her?

On sale 6th July 2001

*Available at most branches of WH Smith, Tesco,
Martins, Borders, Easons, Sainsbury, Woolworth
and most good paperback bookshops* 0601/03b

FREE

4 BOOKS
AND A SURPRISE GIFT!

We would like to take this opportunity to thank you for reading this Mills & Boon® book by offering you the chance to take FOUR more specially selected titles from the Medical Romance™ series absolutely FREE! We're also making this offer to introduce you to the benefits of the Reader Service™—

- ★ FREE home delivery
- ★ FREE monthly Newsletter
- ★ FREE gifts and competitions
- ★ Exclusive Reader Service discounts
- ★ Books available before they're in the shops

Accepting these FREE books and gift places you under no obligation to buy; you may cancel at any time, even after receiving your free shipment. Simply complete your details below and return the entire page to the address below. *You don't even need a stamp!*

YES! Please send me 4 free Medical Romance books and a surprise gift. I understand that unless you hear from me, I will receive 6 superb new titles every month for just £2.49 each, postage and packing free. I am under no obligation to purchase any books and may cancel my subscription at any time. The free books and gift will be mine to keep in any case.

MIZEC

Ms/Mrs/Miss/Mr ....Initials ....

BLOCK CAPITALS PLEASE

Surname ....

Address ....

....

....Postcode ....

Send this whole page to:
UK: FREEPOST CN81, Croydon, CR9 3WZ
EIRE: PO Box 4546, Kilcock, County Kildare (stamp required)